THE TREMENDOUS EVENT

"You don't regret anything, Isabel?" he whispered.

THE
TREMENDOUS EVENT

BY
MAURICE LEBLANC

Translated from the French by
ALEXANDER TEIXEIRA DE MATTOS

100ᵀᴴ ANNIVERSARY COLLECTION
PUBLISHED BY

THE TREMENDOUS EVENT
Copyright ©2021 by SeaWolf Press

PUBLISHED BY SEAWOLF PRESS
All rights reserved. No part of this book may be duplicated in any manner whatsoever without the express written consent of the publisher, except in the form of brief excerpts or quotations used for the purposes of review.
Printed in the U.S.A. on acid-free paper

EDITION INFORMATION
The text is from the 1922 Macaulay edition. The cover is from the first American edition.

SeaWolf Press
P.O. Box 961
Orinda, CA 94563
Email: support@seawolfpress.com
Web: http://www.SeaWolfPress.com

CONTENTS

PART THE FIRST

I	THE SUIT	3
II	THE CROSSING	14
III	GOOD-BYE, SIMON	26
IV	THE GREAT UPHEAVAL	35
V	VIRGIN SOIL	42
VI	TRIUMPH	49
VII	LYNX-EYE	60
VIII	ON THE WAR-PATH	72

PART THE SECOND

I	INSIDE THE WRECK	87
II	ALONG THE CABLE	98
III	SIDE BY SIDE	108
IV	THE BATTLE	116
V	THE CHIEF'S REWARD	126
VI	HELL ON EARTH	138
VII	THE FIGHT FOR THE GOLD	147
VIII	THE HIGH COMMISSIONER	157

AUTHOR'S NOTE

The tremendous event of the 4th. of June, whose consequences affected the relations of the two great Western nations even more profoundly than did the war, has called forth, during the last fifty years, a constant efflorescence of books, memoirs and scientific studies of truthful reports and fabulous narratives. Eye-witnesses have related their impressions; journalists have collected their articles into volumes; scientists have published the results of their researches; novelists have imagined unknown tragedies; and poets have lifted up their voices. There is no detail of that tragic day but has been brought to light; and this is true likewise of the days which went before and of those which came after and of all the reactions, moral or social, economic or political, by which it made itself felt, throughout the twentieth century, in the destinies of the world.

There was nothing lacking but Simon Dubosc's own story. And it was strange that we should have known only by reports, usually fantastic, the part played by the man who, first by chance and then by his indomitable courage and later still by his clear-sighted enthusiasm, was thrust into the very heart of the adventure.

To-day, when the nations are gathered about the statue over-looking the arena in which the hero fought, does it not seem permissible to add to the legend the embellishment of a reality which will not misrepresent it? And, if it is found that this reality trenches too closely upon the man's private life, need we object?

It was in Simon Dubosc that the western spirit first became conscious of itself and it is the whole man that belongs to history.

PART THE FIRST

The Tremendous Event

CHAPTER I

THE SUIT

"Oh, but this is terrible!" cried Simon Dubosc. "Edward, just listen!"

And the young Frenchman, drawing his friend away from the tables arranged in little groups on the terraces of the club-house, showed him, in the late edition of the *Argus*, which a motorcyclist had just brought to the New Golf Club, this telegram, printed in heavy type:

"BOULOGNE, *20 May.*—The master and crew of a fishing-vessel which has returned to harbor declare that this morning, at a spot midway between the French and English coasts, they saw a large steamer lifted up by a gigantic waterspout. After standing on end with her whole length out of the water, she pitched forward and disappeared in the space of a few seconds.

"Such violent eddies followed and the sea, until then quite calm, was affected by such abnormal convulsions that the fishermen had to row their hardest to avoid being dragged into the whirlpool. The naval authorities are sending a couple of tugs to the site of the disaster."

"Well, Rolleston, what do you think of it?"

"Terrible indeed!" replied the Englishman. "Two days ago, the *Ville de Dunkerque*. To-day another ship, and in the same place. There's a coincidence about it. . . ."

"That's precisely what a second telegram says," exclaimed Simon, continuing to read:

"3. O. P. M.—The steamer sunk between Folkestone and Boulogne is the transatlantic liner *Brabant*, of the Rotterdam-Amerika Co., carrying twelve hundred passengers and a crew of eight hundred. No survivors have been picked up. The bodies of the drowned are beginning to rise to the surface.

"There is no doubt that this terrifying calamity, like the loss of the *Ville de Dunkerque* two days ago, was caused by one of those mysterious phenomena which have been disturbing the Straits of Dover during the past week and in which a number of vessels were nearly lost, before the sinking of the *Brabant* and the *Ville de Dunkerque*."

The two young men were silent. Leaning on the balustrade which runs along the terrace of the club-house, they gazed beyond the cliffs at the vast circle of the sea. It was peaceful and kindly innocent of anger or treachery; its near surface was crossed by fine streaks of green or yellow, while, farther out, it was flawless and blue as the sky and, farther still, beneath the motionless cloud, grey as a great sheet of slate.

But, above Brighton, the sun, already dipping towards the downs, shone through the clouds; and a luminous trail of gold-dust appeared upon the sea.

"*La perfide!*" murmured Simon Dubosc. He understood English perfectly, but always spoke French with his friend. "The perfidious brute: how beautiful she is, how attractive! Would you ever have thought her capable of these malevolent whims, which are so destructive and murderous? Are you crossing to-night, Rolleston?"

"Yes, Newhaven to Dieppe."

"You'll be quite safe," said Simon. "The sea has had her two wrecks; she's sated. But why are you in such a hurry to go?"

"I have to interview a crew at Dieppe to-morrow morning; I am putting my yacht in commission. Then, in the afternoon, to Paris, I expect; and, in a week's time, a cruise to Norway. And you, Simon?"

Simon Dubosc did not reply. He had turned toward the club-house, whose windows, in their borders of Virginia creeper and honeysuckle, were blazing with the sun. The players had left the links and were taking tea beneath great many-colored sunshades planted on the lawn. The *Argus* was passing from hand to hand and arousing excited comments. Some of the tables were occupied by young men and women, others by their elders and others by old gentlemen who were recuperating their strength by devouring platefuls of cake and toast.

To the left, beyond the geranium-beds, the gentle undulations of the links began, covered with turf that was like green velvet; and right at the end, a long way off, rose the tall figure of a last player, escorted by his two caddies.

"Lord Bakefield's daughter and her three friends can't take their eyes off you," said Rolleston.

Simon smiled:

"Miss Bakefield is looking at me because she knows I love her; and her three friends because they know I love Miss Bakefield. A man in love is always something to look at; a pleasant sight for the one who is loved and an irritating sight for those who are not."

This was spoken without a trace of vanity. For that matter, no man could have possessed more natural charm or displayed a more alluring simplicity. The expression of his face, his blue eyes, his smile and something personal, an emanation compounded of strength and suppleness and healthy gaiety, of confidence in himself and in life, all contributed to give this peculiarly favored young man a power of attraction to whose spell the onlooker readily surrendered.

Devoted to out-door games and exercises, he had grown to manhood with those young postwar Frenchmen who made a strong point of physical culture and a rational mode of life. His movements and his attitudes alike revealed that harmony which is developed by a logical training and is still further refined, in those who comply with the rules of a very active intellectual existence, by the study of art and a feeling for beauty in all of its forms.

For him, indeed, as for many others, liberation from the lecture-room had not meant the beginning of a new life. If, by reason of a superfluity of energy, he was impelled to give much of his time to games and to attempts at establishing records which took him to all the running-grounds and athletic battle-fields of Europe and America, he never allowed his body to take precedence of his mind. Every day, come what might, he set apart the two or three hours of solitude, of reading and meditation, which the intellect requires for its nourishment, continuing to learn with the enthusiasm of a student who is prolonging the life of the school and university until events compel him to make a choice among the paths which he has opened up for himself.

His father, to whom he was bound by ties of the liveliest affection, was puzzled:

"After all, Simon, what are you aiming at? What's your object?"

"I am training."

"For what?"

"I don't know. But an hour strikes for each of us when we must be fully prepared, well equipped, with our ideas in good order and our muscles absolutely fit. I shall be ready."

And so he reached his thirtieth year. It was at the beginning of that year, at Nice, through Edward Rolleston, that he made Miss Bakefield's acquaintance.

"I am sure to see your father at Dieppe," said Rolleston. "He will be surprised that you haven't returned with me, as we arranged last month. What shall I say to him?"

"Say that I'm stopping here a little longer . . . or no, don't say anything. . . . I'll write to him . . . to-morrow perhaps . . . or the day after. . . ."

He took Rolleston's arm:

"Tell me, old chap," he said, "tell me. If I were to ask Lord Bakefield for his daughter's hand, what do you think would happen?"

Rolleston appeared to be nonplussed. He hesitated and then replied:

"Miss Bakefield's father is a peer, and perhaps you don't know that her mother, the wonderful Lady Constance, who died some six years ago, was the grand-daughter of a son of George III. Therefore she had an eighth part of blood royal running in her veins."

Edward Rolleston pronounced these words with such unction that Simon, the irreverent Frenchman, could not help laughing:

"The deuce! An eighth! So that Miss Bakefield can still boast a sixteenth part and her children will enjoy a thirty-second! My chances are diminishing! In the matter of blood royal, the most that I can lay claim to is a great-grandfather, a pork-butcher by trade, who voted for the death of Louis XVI.! That doesn't amount to much!"

He gave his friend a gentle push:

"Do me a service. Miss Bakefield is alone for the moment. Keep her friends engaged so that I can speak to her for a minute or two: I shan't be longer."

Edward Rolleston, a friend of Simon's who shared his athletic tastes, was a tall young man, too pale, too thin and so long in the back that he had acquired a stoop. Simon knew that he had many faults, including a love of whisky and the habit of haunting private bars and living by his wits. But he was a devoted friend, in whom Simon was conscious of a genuine and loyal affection.

The two men went forward together. Miss Bakefield came to meet Simon, while Rolleston accosted her three friends.

Miss Bakefield wore an absolutely simple wash frock, without any of the trimmings that were then the fashion. Her bare throat, her arms, which showed through the muslin of her sleeves, her face and even her forehead under her hat were of that warm tint which the skin of some fair-haired women acquires in the sun and the open air. Her eyes were almost black, flecked with glittering specks of gold. Her hair, which shone with metallic glints, was dressed low on the neck in a heavy coil. But these were trivial details which you noted only at leisure, when you had in some degree recovered from the glorious spectacle of her beauty in all its completeness.

Simon had not so recovered. He always paled a little when he met Miss Bakefield's eyes, however tenderly they rested on him.

"Isabel," he said, "are you determined?"

"Quite as much as yesterday," she said, smiling; "and I shall be still more so to-morrow, when the moment comes for action."

"Still. . . . We have known each other hardly four months."

"Meaning thereby? . . ."

"Meaning that, now that we are about to perform an irreparable action, I invite you to use your judgment. . . ."

"Rather than listen to my love? Since I first loved you, Simon, I have not been able to discover the least disagreement between my judgment and my love. That's why I am going with you to-morrow morning."

"Isabel!"

"Would you rather that I left to-morrow night with my father? On a voyage lasting three or four years? That is what he proposes, what he insists upon. It's for you to choose."

While they exchanged these serious words, their faces displayed no trace of the emotion which thrilled the very depths of their beings. It was as though, in being together, they experienced that sense of happiness which gives strength and tranquillity. And, as the girl, like Simon, was tall and bore herself magnificently, they received a vague impression that they were one of those privileged couples whom destiny selects for a life more strenuous, nobler and more passionate than the ordinary.

"Very well," said Simon. "But let me at least appeal to your father. He doesn't know. . . ."

"There is nothing he doesn't know, Simon. And it is precisely because our love displeases him and displeases my step-mother even more that he wants to get me away from you."

"I insist on this, Isabel."

"Speak to him, then, Simon, and, if he refuses, don't try to see me to-day. To-morrow, a little before twelve o'clock, I shall be at Newhaven. Wait for me by the gangway of the steamer."

He had something more to say:

"Have you seen the *Argus*?"

"Yes."

"You're not frightened of the crossing?"

She smiled. He bowed over her hand and kissed it and said no more.

Lord Bakefield, a peer of the United Kingdom, had been married first to the aforesaid great-grand-daughter of George III. and secondly to the Duchess of Faulconbridge. He was the owner, in his own right or his wife's, of country-houses, estates and town properties which enabled him to travel from Brighton to Folkestone almost without leaving his own domains. He was the distant player who had lingered on the links; and his figure, now less remote, was appearing and disappearing according to the lay of the ground. Simon decided to profit by the occasion and to go to meet him.

He set out resolutely. In spite of the young girl's warning and though he had learnt, from her and from Edward Rolleston, something of Lord Bakefield's true character and of his prejudices, he was influenced by the memory of the cordial welcome which Isabel's father had invariably accorded him hitherto.

This time again the grip of his hand was full of geniality. Lord Bakefield's face—a round face, too fat for his thin and lanky body, too florid and a little commonplace, though not lacking in intelligence—lit up with satisfaction.

"Well, young man, I suppose you have come to say good-bye? You have heard that we are leaving?"

"I have, Lord Bakefield; and that is why I should like a few words with you."

"Quite, quite! You have my attention."

He bent over the tee, building up, with his two hands, a little mound of sand on whose summit he placed his ball; then, drawing himself up, he accepted the brassy which one of his caddies held out to him and took his stand, perfectly poised, with his left foot a little advanced and his knees very slightly bent. Two or three trial swings, to assure himself of the precise direction; a second's reflection and calculation; and suddenly the club swung upwards, descended and struck the ball.

The ball flew through the air and suddenly veered to the left; then, curving to the right after passing a clump of trees which formed an obstacle to be avoided, it fell on the putting-green at a few yards' distance from the hole.

"Well done!" cried Simon. "A very pretty screw!"

"Not so bad, not so bad," said Lord Bakefield, resuming his round.

Simon did not allow himself to be disconcerted by this curious method of beginning an interview and broached his subject, without further preamble:

"Lord Bakefield, you know who my father is, a Dieppe shipowner, with the largest merchant-fleet in France. So I need say no more on that side."

"Capital fellow, M. Dubosc," said Lord Bakefield, approvingly. "I had the pleasure of shaking hands with him at Dieppe last month. Capital fellow."

Simon continued, delightedly:

"Let us consider my own case. I'm an only son. I have an independent fortune from my poor mother. When I was twenty, I crossed the Sahara in an aeroplane without touching ground. At twenty-one, I made the record for the running mile. At twenty-two, I won two events at the Olympic Games: fencing and swimming. At twenty-five, I was the world's champion all-round athlete. And mixed up with all this was the Morocco campaign: four times mentioned in dispatches, promoted lieutenant in the reserve, awarded the military medal and the medal for saving life. That's all. Oh no, I was forgetting: licentiate in letters, laureate of the Academy for my essays on the Grecian ideal of beauty. There you are. I am twenty-nine years of age."

Lord Bakefield looked at him with the tail of his eye and murmured:

"Not bad, young man, not bad."

"As for the future," Simon continued, without waiting, "that won't take long. I don't like making plans. However, I have the offer of a seat in the Chamber of Deputies at the coming elections, in August. Of course, politics don't much interest me. But after all . . . if I must. . . . And then I'm young: I shall always manage to get a place in the sun. Only, there's one thing . . . at least, from your point of view, Lord Bakefield. My name is Simon Dubosc. Dubosc in one word, without the particle . . . without the least semblance of a title. . . . And that, of course. . . ."

He expressed himself without embarrassment, in a good-humoured, playful tone. Lord Bakefield, the picture of amiability, was quite imperturbed. Simon broke into a laugh:

"I quite grasp the situation; and I would much rather give you a more elaborate pedigree, with a coat-of-arms, motto and title-deeds complete. Unfortunately, that's impossible. However, if it comes to that, we can trace back our ancestry to the fourteenth century. Yes, Lord Bakefield, in 1392, Mathieu Dubosc, a yeoman in the manor of Blancmesnil, near Dieppe, was sentenced to fifty strokes of the rod for theft. And the Duboscs went on valiantly tilling the soil, from father to son. The farm still exists, the farm *du Bosc*, that is *du Bosquet*, of the clump of trees. . . ."

"Yes, yes, I know," interrupted Lord Bakefield.

"Oh, you know," repeated the younger man, somewhat taken back.

He intuitively felt, by the old nobleman's attitude and the very tone of the interruption, the full importance of the words which he was about to hear.

And Lord Bakefield continued:

"Yes, I happen to know. . . . When I was at Dieppe last month, I made a few inquiries about my family, which sprang from Normandy. Bakefield as you may perhaps not be aware, is the English corruption of Bacqueville. There was a Bacqueville among the companions of William the Conqueror. You know the picturesque little market-town of that name in the middle of the Pays de Caux? Well, there is a fourteenth-century deed in the records at Bacqueville, a deed signed in London, by which the Count of Bacqueville, Baron of Auppegard and Gourel, grants to his vassal, the Lord of Blancmesnil, the right of administering justice on the farm du Bosc ... the same farm du Bosc on which poor Mathieu received his thrashing. An amusing coincidence, very amusing indeed: what do you think, young man?"

This time, Simon was pierced to the quick. It was impossible to imagine a more impertinent answer couched in more frank and courteous terms. Quite baldly, under the pretence of telling a genealogical anecdote, Lord Bakefield made it clear that in his eyes young Dubosc was of scarcely greater importance than was the fourteenth-century yeoman in the eyes of the mighty English Baron Bakefield and feudal lord of Blancmesnil. The titles and exploits of Simon Dubosc, world's champion, victor in the Olympic Games, laureate of the French Academy and all-round athlete, did not weigh an ounce in the scale by which a British peer, conscious of his superiority, judges the merits of those who aspire to his daughter's hand. Now the merits of Simon Dubosc were of the kind which are amply rewarded with the favor of an assumed politeness and a cordial handshake.

All this was so evident and the old nobleman's mind, with its pride, its prejudice and its stiff-necked obstinacy, stood so plainly revealed that Simon, who was unwilling to suffer the humiliation of a refusal, replied in a rather impertinent and bantering tone:

"Needless to say, Lord Bakefield, I make no pretension to becoming your son-in-law just like that, all in a moment and without having done something to deserve so immense a privilege. My request refers first of all to the conditions which Simon Dubosc, the yeoman's descendant, would have to fulfil to obtain the hand of a Bakefield. I presume that, as the Bakefields have an ancestor who came over with William the Conqueror, Simon Dubosc, to rehabilitate himself in their eyes, would have to conquer something—such as a kingdom—or, following the Bastard's example, to make a triumphant descent upon England? Is that the way of it?"

"More or less, young man," replied the old peer, slightly disconcerted by this attack.

"Perhaps too," continued Simon, "he ought to perform a few superhuman actions, a few feats of prowess of world-wide importance, affecting the happiness of mankind? William the Conqueror first, Hercules or Don Quixote next? . . . Then, perhaps, one might come to terms?"

"One might, young man."

"And that would be all?"

"Not quite!"

And Lord Bakefield, who had recovered his self-possession, continued, in a genial fashion:

"I cannot undertake that Isabel would remain free for very long. You would have to succeed within a given space of time. Do you consider, M. Dubosc, that I shall be too exacting if I fix this period at two months?"

"You are much too generous, Lord Bakefield," cried Simon. "Three weeks will be ample. Think of it: three weeks to prove myself the equal of William the Conqueror and the rival of Don Quixote! It is longer than I need! I thank you from the bottom of my heart! For the present, Lord Bakefield, good-bye!"

And, turning on his heels, fairly well-satisfied with an interview which, after all, released him from any obligation to the old nobleman, Simon Dubosc returned to the club-house. Isabel's name had hardly been mentioned.

"Well," asked Rolleston, "have you put forward your suit?"

"More or less."

"And what was the reply?"

"Couldn't be better, Edward, couldn't be better! It is not at all impossible that the decent man whom you see over there, knocking a little ball into a little hole, may become the father-in-law of Simon Dubosc. A mere nothing would do the trick: some tremendous stupendous event which would change the face of the earth. That's all."

"Events of that sort are rare, Simon," said Rolleston.

"Then, my dear Rolleston, things must happen as Isabel and I have decided."

"And that is?"

Simon did not reply. He had caught sight of Isabel, who was leaving the club-house.

On seeing him, she stopped short. She stood some twenty paces away, grave and smiling. And in the glance which they exchanged there was all the tenderness, devotion, happiness and certainty that two young people, can promise each other on the threshold of life.

CHAPTER II

THE CROSSING

Next day, at Newhaven, Simon Dubosc learnt that, at about six o'clock on the previous evening, a fishing-smack with a crew of eight hands had foundered in sight of Seaford. The cyclone had been seen from the shore.

"Well, captain," asked Simon, who happened to know the first officer of the boat which was about to cross that day, having met him in Dieppe, "well captain, what do you make of it? More wrecks! Don't you think things are beginning to get alarming?"

"It looks like it, worse luck!" replied the captain. "Fifteen passengers have refused to come on board. They're frightened. Yet, after all, one has to take chances...."

"Chances which keep on recurring, captain, and over the whole of the Channel just now...."

"M. Dubosc, if you take the whole of the Channel, you will probably find several hundred craft afloat at one time. Each of them runs a risk, but you'll admit the risk is small."

"Was the crossing good last night?" asked Simon, thinking of his friend Rolleston.

"Very good, both ways, and so will ours be. The *Queen Mary* is a fast boat; she does the sixty-four miles in just under two hours. We shall leave and we shall arrive; you may be sure of that, M. Dubosc."

The captain's confidence, while reassuring Simon, did not completely allay the fears which would not even have entered his mind in ordinary times. He selected two cabins separated by a stateroom. Then, as he still had twenty-five minutes to wait, he repaired to the harbor station.

There he found people greatly excited. At the booking-office, at the refreshment-bar and in the waiting-room where the latest telegrams were written on a black-board, travellers with anxious faces were hurrying to and fro. Groups collected about persons who were better-informed than the rest and who were talking very loudly and gesticulating. A number of passengers were demanding repayment of the price of their tickets.

"Why, there's Old Sandstone!" said Simon to himself, as he recognized one of his former professors at a table in the refreshment-room.

And, instead of avoiding him, as he commonly did when the worthy man appeared at the corner of some street in Dieppe, he went up to him and took a seat beside him:

"Well, my dear professor, how goes it?"

"What, is that you, Dubosc?"

Beneath a silk hat of an antiquated shape and rusty with age was a round, fat face like a village priest's, a face with enormous cheeks which overlapped a collar of doubtful cleanliness. Something like a bit of black braid did duty as a necktie. The waist-coat and frock-coat were adorned with stains; and the over-coat, of a faded green, had three of its four buttons missing and acknowledged an age even more venerable than that of the hat.

Old Sandstone—he was never known except by this nickname—had taught natural science at Dieppe College for the last twenty-five years. A geologist first and foremost and a geologist of real merit, he owed his by-name to his investigations of the sedimentary formations of the Norman coast, investigations which he had extended even to the bottom of the sea and which, though he was nearly sixty years of age, he was still continuing with unabated enthusiasm. Only last year, in the month of September, Simon had seen him, a big, heavy man, bloated with fat and crippled with rheumatism, struggling into a diver's dress and making, within sight of Saint-Valéry-en-Caux, his forty-eighth descent. The Channel from Le Havre to Dunkirk and from Portsmouth to Dover, no longer had any secrets for him.

"Are you going back to Dieppe presently, professor?"

"On the contrary, I have just come from Dieppe. I crossed last night, as soon as I heard of the wreck of the English fishing-smack, you know, between Seaford and Cuckmere Haven. I have already begun to make inquiries this morning, of some people who were visiting the Roman camp and saw the thing happen."

"Well?" said Simon, eagerly.

"Well, they saw, at a mile from the coast, a whirl of waves and foam revolving at a dizzy speed round a hollow centre. Then suddenly a column of water gushed straight up, mixed with sand and stones, and fell back on all sides, like a rain of rockets. It was magnificent!"

"And the fishing-smack?"

"The fishing-smack?" echoed Old Sandstone, who seemed not to understand, to take no interest in this trivial detail. "Oh, yes, the fishing-smack, of course! Well, she disappeared, that's all!"

The young man was silent, but the next moment continued:

"Now my dear professor, tell me frankly, do you think there's any danger in crossing?"

"Oh, that's absurd! It's as though you were to ask me whether one ought to shut one's self in one's room when there is a thunderstorm. Of course the lightning strikes the earth now and again. But there's plenty of margin all round. . . . Besides, aren't you a good swimmer? Well, at the least sign of danger, dive into the sea without delay: don't stop to think; just dive!"

"And what is your opinion, professor? How do you explain all these phenomena?"

"How? Oh, very simply! I will remind you, to begin with, that in 1912 the Somme experienced a few shocks which amounted to actual earthquakes. Point number one. Secondly, these shocks coincided with local disturbances in the Channel, which passed almost unnoticed; but they attracted my attention and were the starting point of all my recent investigations. Among others, one of these disturbances in which I am inclined to see the premonitory signs of the present water-spouts, occurred off Saint-Valéry. And that was why you caught me one day, I remember, going down in a diving-suit just at that spot. Now, from all this, it follows. . . ."

"What follows?"

Old Sandstone interrupted himself, seized the young man's hand and suddenly changed the course of the conversation:

"Now tell me, Dubosc," he said, "have you read my pamphlet on *The Cliffs of the Channel*? You haven't, have you? Well, if you had, you would know that one of the chapters, entitled, '*What will occur in the Channel in the year 2000*,' is now being fulfilled. D'you understand? I predicted the whole thing! Not these minor incidents of wrecks and water-spouts, of course, but what they seem to announce. Yes, Dubosc; whether it be in the year 2000, or the year 3000, or next week, I have foretold in all its details the unheard-of, astounding, yet very natural thing which will happen sooner or later."

He had now grown animated. Drops of sweat beaded his cheeks and forehead; and, taking from an inner pocket of his frock-coat a long narrow wallet, with a lock to it and so much worn and so often repaired that its appearance harmonized perfectly with his green over-coat and his rusty hat:

"You want to know the truth?" he exclaimed. "It's here. All my observations and all my hypotheses are contained in this wallet."

And he was inserting the key in the lock when loud voices were raised on the platform. The tables in the refreshment-room were at once deserted. Without paying further heed to Old Sandstone, Simon followed the crowd which was rushing into the waiting-room.

Two telegrams had come from France. One, after reporting the wreck of a coasting-vessel, the *Bonne Vierge*, which plied weekly between Calais, Le Havre and Cherbourg, announced that the Channel Tunnel had fallen in, fortunately without the loss of a single life. The other, which the crowd read as it was being written, stated that "the keeper of the Ailly lighthouse, near Dieppe, had at break of day seen five columns of water and sand shooting up almost simultaneously, two miles from the coast, and stirring up the sea between Veules and Pourville."

These telegrams elicited cries of dismay. The destruction of the Channel Tunnel, ten years of effort wasted, millions of pounds swallowed up: this was evidently a calamity! But how much more dreadful was the sinister wording of the second telegram! Veules! Pourville! Dieppe! That was the coast which they would have to make for! The steamboat, in two hours' time, would be entering the very region affected by the cataclysm! On sailing, Seaford and Hastings; on nearing port, Veules, Pourville and Dieppe!

There was a rush for the booking-office. The station-master's and inspectors' offices were besieged. Two hundred people rushed on board the vessel to recover their trunks and bags; and a crowd of distraught travellers, staggering under the weight of their luggage, took the up-train by assault, as though the sea-walls and the quays and rampart of the cliffs were unable to protect them from the hideous catastrophe.

Simon shuddered. He could not but be impressed by the fears displayed by these people. And then what was the meaning of this mysterious sequence of phenomena, which seemed incapable of any natural explanation? What invisible tempest was making the waves boil up from the depths of a motionless sea? Why did these sudden cyclones all occur within so small a radius, affecting only a limited region?

All around him the tumult increased, amid repeated painful scenes. One of these he found particularly distressing; for the people concerned were French and he was better able to understand what they were saying. There was a family, consisting of the father and mother, both still young, and their six children, the smallest of whom, only a few months old, was sleeping in its mother's arms. And the mother was imploring her husband in a sort of despair:

"Don't let us go, please don't let us go! We're not obliged to!"

"But we are, my dear: you saw my partner's letter. And really there's no occasion for all this distress!"

"Please, darling! . . . I have a presentiment. . . . You know I'm always right. . . ."

"Would you rather I crossed alone?"

"Oh no! Not that!"

Simon heard no more. But he was never to forget that cry of a loving wife, nor the grief-stricken expression of the mother who, at that moment, was embracing her six children with a glance.

He made his escape. The clock pointed to half-past eleven; and Miss Bakefield ought to be on her way. But, when he reached the quay, he saw a motor-car turning the corner of a street; and at the window of the car was Isabel's golden head. In a moment all his gloomy thoughts were banished. He had not expected the girl for another twenty minutes; and, though he was not afraid of suffering, he had made up his mind that those last twenty minutes would be a period of distress and anxiety. Would she keep her promise? Might she not meet with some unforeseen obstacle? . . . And here was Isabel arriving!

Yesterday he had determined, as a measure of precaution, not to speak to her until they had taken their places on the boat. However, as soon as Simon saw her step out of the car, he ran to meet her. She was wrapped in a grey cloak and carried a rug rolled in a strap. A sailor followed with her travelling-bag.

"Excuse me, Isabel," said Simon, "but something so serious has happened that I am bound to consult you. The telegrams, in fact, mention a whole series of catastrophes which have occurred precisely in the part which we shall have to cross."

Isabel did not seem much put out:

"You're saying this, Simon, in a very calm tone which does not match your words at all."

"It's because I'm so happy!" he murmured.

Their eyes met in a long and penetrating glance. Then she continued:

"What would you do, Simon, if you were alone?"

And, when he hesitated what to answer:

"You would go," she said. "And so should I. . . ."

She stepped onto the gangway.

Half an hour later, the *Queen Mary* left Newhaven harbor. At that instant, Simon, who was always so completely his own master and who, even in the most feverish moments of enthusiasm, claimed the power of controlling his emotions, felt his legs trembling beneath him, while his eyes grew moist with tears. The test of happiness was too much for him.

Simon had never been in love before. Love was an event which he awaited at his leisure; and he did not think it essential to prepare for its coming by seeking it in adventures which might well exhaust his ardor:

"Love," he used to say, "should blend with life, should form a part of life and not be added to it. Love is not an aim in itself: it is a principle of action and the noblest in the world."

From the first day when he saw her, Isabel's beauty had dazzled him; and he needed very little time to discover that, until the last moment of his life, no other woman would ever mean anything to him. The same irresistible and deliberate impulse drove Isabel towards Simon. Brought up in the south of France, speaking French as her native tongue, she did not feel and did not evoke in Simon the sense of embarrassment that almost invariably arises from a difference of nationality. That which united them was infinitely stronger than that which divided them.

It was a curious thing, but during these past four months, while love was blossoming within them like a plant whose flowers were constantly renewed and constantly increasing in beauty, they had had none of those long conversations in which lovers eagerly question each other and in which each seeks to find entrance into the unknown territory of the other's soul. They spoke little and rarely of themselves, as though they had delegated to gentle daily life the task of raising the veils of the mystery one by one.

Simon knew only that Isabel was not happy. After losing at the age of fifteen a mother whom she adored, she failed to find in her father the love and the caresses that might have consoled her. Moreover, Lord Bakefield almost immediately fell under the dominion of the Duchess of Faulconbridge, a vain, tyrannical woman, who rarely stirred from her villa at Cannes or her country-seat near Battle, but whose malign influence exerted itself equally close at hand and far away, in speech and by letter, on her husband and on her step-daughter, whom she persecuted with her morbid jealousy.

Naturally enough, Isabel and Simon exchanged a mutual promise. And, naturally enough, on coming into collision with Lord Bakefield's implacable will and his wife's hatred, they arrived at the only possible solution, that of running away. This was proposed without heroic phrases and adopted without any painful struggle or reluctance. Each formed a decision in perfect liberty. To themselves their action appeared extremely simple. Loyally determined to prolong their engagement until the moment when all obstacles would be smoothed away, they faced the future like travellers turning to a radiant and hospitable country.

In the open Channel a choppy sea was beginning to rise before a steady light breeze. In the west the clouds were mustering in battle array, but they were distant enough to promise a calm passage in glorious sunshine. Indifferent to the assault of the waves, the vessel sped straight for her port, as though no power existed which could have turned her aside from her strict course.

Isabel and Simon were seated on one of the benches on the after deck. The girl had taken off her cloak and hat and offered to the wind her arms and shoulders, protected only by a cambric blouse.

Nothing more beautiful could be imagined than the play of the sunlight on the gold of her hair. Though grave and dreamy, she was radiant with youth and happiness. Simon gazed at her in an ecstasy of admiration:

"You don't regret anything, Isabel?" he whispered.

"No!"

"You're not frightened?"

"Why should I be, with you? There is nothing to threaten us."

Simon pointed to the sea:

"That will, perhaps."

"No!"

He told her of his conversation with Lord Bakefield on the previous day and of the three conditions upon which they had agreed. She was amused, and asked him:

"May I too lay down a condition?"

"What condition, Isabel?"

"Fidelity," she replied, gravely. "Absolute fidelity. No lapses! I could never forgive anything of that sort."

He kissed her hand and said:

"There is no love without fidelity. I love you."

There were few people around them, for the panic had affected mainly the first-class passengers. But, apart from the two lovers, all those who had persisted in crossing betrayed by some sign their secret uneasiness or their alarm. On the right were two old, very old clergymen, accompanied by a third, a good deal younger. These three remained unmoved, worthy brothers of the heroes who sang hymns on the sinking *Titanic*. Nevertheless, their hands were folded as though in prayer. On the left was the French couple whose conversation Dubosc had overheard. The young father and mother, leaning closely on each other, searched the horizon with fevered eyes. Four boys, the four older children, all strong and robust, their cheeks ruddy with health, were coming and going, in search of information which they immediately brought back with them. A little girl sat crying at her parents' feet, without saying a word. The mother was nursing the sixth child, which from time to time turned to Isabel and smiled at her.

Meanwhile, the breeze was growing colder. Simon leant toward his companion:

"You're not feeling chilly, Isabel?" he said.

"No, I'm used to it. . . ."

"Still, though you left your bag below you brought your rug on deck, very wisely. Why don't you undo it?"

The rug was still rolled up in its straps; and Isabel had even passed one of the straps around an iron rod, which fastened the bench to the deck, and buckled it.

"My bag contains nothing of value," she said.

"Nor the rug, I presume?"

"Yes, it does."

"Really? What?"

"A miniature to which my poor mother was very much attached, because it is a portrait of her grandmother painted for George III."

"It has just a sentimental value, therefore?"

"Oh dear no! My mother had it set in all her finest pearls, which gives it an inestimable value to-day. Thinking of the future, she left me, in this way, a fortune of my own."

Simon laughed:

"And that's the safe!"

"Yes, that's the safe!" she said, joining in his laughter. "The miniature is pinned to the middle of the rug, between the straps where no one would think of looking for it. You're laughing, but I am superstitious where that miniature is concerned. It's a sort of talisman. . . ."

For some time they spoke no further. The coast had disappeared from sight. The swell was increasing and the *Queen Mary* was rolling a little.

At this moment they were passing a beautiful white yacht.

"That's the Comte de Bauge's *Castor*," cried one of the four boys. "She's on her way to Dieppe."

Two ladies and two gentlemen were lunching under an awning, Isabel bowed her head so as to hide her face.

This thoughtless movement displeased her; for, a moment later, she said (and all the words which they exchanged during these few minutes were to remain engraved on their memories):

"Simon, you really believe, don't you, that I was entitled to leave home?"

"Why," he exclaimed, in surprise, "don't we love each other?"

"Yes, we love each other," she murmured. "And then there's the life which I was leading with a woman whose one delight was to insult my mother. . . ."

She said no more. Simon had laid his hand on hers and nothing could reassure her more effectually than the fondness of that pressure.

The four boys, who had disappeared again, came running back:

"You can see the company's mail-boat that left Dieppe at the same time that we left Newhaven. She's called the *Pays de Caux*. We shall pass her in a quarter of an hour. So you see, mama, there's no danger."

"Yes, but it's afterwards, when we get closer to Dieppe."

"Why?" objected her husband. "The other boat hasn't signalled anything extraordinary. The danger is altering its position, moving farther away. . . ."

The mother made no reply. Her face retained the same piteous expression. The little girl at her knee was still silently crying.

The captain passed Simon and saluted.

And a few more minutes elapsed.

Simon was whispering words of love which Isabel did not catch very distinctly. The little girl's constant tears were causing her some distress.

Shortly after, a gust of wind made the waves leap higher. Here and there streaks of white, seething foam appeared. There was nothing remarkable in this, as the wind was gaining in force and lashing the crests of the waves. But why did these foaming billows appear only in one part and that precisely the part which they were about to cross?

The father and mother had risen to their feet. Other passengers were leaning over the rails. The captain was seen running up the poop-steps.

And it came suddenly, in a moment.

Before Isabel and Simon, sitting self-absorbed, had the least idea of what was happening, a frightful clamor, made up of a thousand shrieks, rose from all parts of the boat, from port and starboard, from stem to stern, even from below; from every side, as though the minds of all had been obsessed by the possibility of disaster, as though all eyes, from the moment of departure, had been watching for the slightest premonitory sign.

A monstrous sight. Three hundred yards ahead, as though in the centre of a target at which the bows of the vessel were aimed, a hideous fountain had burst from the surface of the sea, bombarding the sky with masses of rock, blocks of lava and flying masses of spray, which fell back into a circle of foaming breakers and yawning whirlpools. And a wind of hurricane force gyrated above this chaos, bellowing like a bull.

Suddenly silence fell upon the paralysed crowd, the deathly silence that precedes an inevitable catastrophe. Then, yonder, a rattle of thunder that rent the air. Then the voice of the captain at his post, roaring out his orders, trying to shout down the monster's myriad voices.

For a moment there seemed some hope of salvation. The vessel put forth so great an effort that she appeared to be gliding along a tangent away from the infernal circle into which she was on the point of being drawn. But it was a vain hope! The circle seemed to be increasing in size. Its outer waves were approaching. A mass of rock crushed one of the funnels.

And again there were shrieks, followed by a panic and an insane rush for the life-boats; already some of the passengers were fighting for places. . . .

Simon did not hesitate. Isabel was a good swimmer. They must make the attempt.

"Come!" he said. The girl, standing beside him, had flung her arms about him. "We can't stay here! Come!"

And, when she struggled, instinctively resisting the course which he had proposed, he took a firmer hold of her.

She entreated him:

"Oh, it's horrible . . . all these children . . . the little girl crying! . . . Couldn't we save them?"

"Come!" he repeated, in a masterful tone.

She still resisted him. Then he took her head in his two hands and kissed her on the lips:

"Come, my darling, come!"

The girl fainted. He lifted her in his arms and threw one leg over the rail:

"Don't be afraid!" he said. "I will answer for your life!"

"I am not afraid," she said. "I am not afraid with you...."

They leapt into the water.

CHAPTER III

GOOD-BYE, SIMON

Twenty minutes later, they were picked up by the *Castor*, the yacht which by this time had passed the *Queen Mary*. As for the *Pays de Caux*, the steamer sailing from Dieppe, subsequent enquiries proved that the passengers and the crew had compelled the captain to flee from the scene of the disaster. The sight of the huge waterspout, the spectacle of the ship lifting her stern out of the waves, rearing up bodily and falling back as though into the mouth of a funnel, the upheaval of the sea, which seemed to have given way beneath the assault of maniacal forces and which, within the circumference of the frenzied circle, revolved upon itself in a sort of madness: all this was so terrifying that women fainted and men threatened the captain with their levelled revolvers.

The *Castor* also had begun by fleeing the spot. But the Conte de Bauge, detecting through his field-glasses the handkerchief which Simon was waving, persuaded his sailors, despite the desperate opposition of his friends, to put about, while avoiding contact with the dangerous zone.

For that matter, the sea was subsiding. The eruption had lasted less than a minute; and it was as though the monster was now resting, sated, content with its meal, like a beast of prey after its kill. The squall had passed. The whirlpool broke up into warring currents which opposed and annulled one another. There were no more breakers, no more foam. Beneath the great undulating shroud which the little waves, tossing in harmless frolic, spread above the sunken vessel, the tragedy of five hundred death-struggles was consummated.

Under these conditions, the rescue was an easy task. Isabel and Simon, who could have held out for hours longer, were taken to the two cabins and supplied with a change of clothing. Isabel had not even lost consciousness. The yacht sailed away immediately. Those on board were eager to escape from the accursed circle. The sudden subsidence of the sea seemed as dangerous as its fury.

Nothing occurred before they reached the French coast. The oppressive, menacing lull continued. Simon Dubosc, directly he had changed his clothes, joined the count and his party. A little embarrassed in respect of Miss Bakefield, he spoke of her as a friend whom he had met by chance on the *Queen Mary* and by whose side he had found himself at the moment of the catastrophe.

For the rest, he was not questioned. The company on board the yacht were still profoundly uneasy; the thought of what might happen obsessed them. Further events were preparing. All had the impression that an invisible enemy was prowling stealthily around them.

Twice Simon went below to Isabel's cabin. The door was closed and there was no sound from within. But Simon knew that Isabel, though she had recovered from her fatigue and was already forgetting the dangers which had threatened them, nevertheless could not shake off the horror of what she had seen. He himself was still terribly depressed, haunted by the vision so frightful that it seemed the extravagant image of a nightmare rather than the memory of an actual thing. Was it true that they had one and all lost their lives: the three clergymen with their austere faces, the four happy, cheerful boys, their father and mother, the little girl who had cried, the child that had smiled at Isabel, the captain and every single individual of all those who had covered the *Queen Mary's* decks?

About four o'clock, the clouds, unrolling in blacker and denser masses, had conquered the heavens. Already the watchers felt the first breath of the great squalls whose precipitous onset was at hand, whose battalions, let loose across the Atlantic, were about to rush into the narrow straits of the Channel and mingle their devastating efforts with the mysterious forces rising from the depths of the sea. The horizon was blotted out as the clouds released their contents.

But the yacht was nearing Dieppe. The Count and Simon Dubosc, each gazing through a pair of binoculars, cried out as with one voice, struck at the same moment by the most unexpected sight. Looking at the row of buildings, which line the long sea-front like a tall rampart of brick and stone, they could plainly see that the roof and upper storey of the two largest hotels, the Imperial and the Astoria, situated in the middle, had collapsed. And the next instant they caught sight of other houses which were tottering, leaning forward, fissured and half-demolished.

Suddenly a flame shot up from one of these houses. In a few minutes there was a violent outbreak of fire; and on every side, from one end of the sea-front to the other, a panic-stricken crowd, whose shouts they could hear, came pouring down the streets and running to the beach.

"There is no doubt about it," spluttered the Count. "There has been an earthquake, a very violent shock, which must have synchronized with the sort of waterspout in which the *Queen Mary* disappeared."

When nearer, they saw that the sea must have risen, sweeping over the sea-wall, for long streaks of mud marked the lawns, while the beach to right and left was covered with stranded shipping.

And they saw too that the end of the jetty and the light-house had disappeared, that the breakwater had been carried away and that boats were drifting about the harbor.

The wireless telegram announcing the wreck of the *Queen Mary* had redoubled the panic. No one dared fly from the peril on land by taking to the open sea. The relatives of the passengers stood massed together, in witless and hopeless waiting, on the landing stage and what remained of the jetty.

In the midst of all this turmoil, the yacht's arrival passed almost unperceived. Each was living for himself, without curiosity, heedless of all but his own danger and that of his kinsfolk. A few distraught journalists were darting about feverishly for news; and the port-authorities subjected Simon and the Count to a hasty and perfunctory enquiry. Simon evaded their questions as far as possible. Once free, he escorted Isabel to the nearest hotel, saw her comfortably settled and asked her for permission to go in search of information. He was uneasy, for he believed his father to be in Dieppe.

The Duboscs' house stood at the first turning on the great slope which climbs to the top of the cliffs on the left, itself hidden behind a clump of trees and covered with flowers and creepers, it had a series of terraced gardens which overlooked the town and the sea. Simon was at once reassured on learning that his father was in Paris and would not be home until next day. He was also told that they had felt only a slight shake on this side of Dieppe.

He therefore went back to Isabel's hotel. She was still in her room, however, needing rest, and sent down word that she would rather be alone until the evening. Somewhat astonished by this reply, the full meaning of which he was not to understand till later, he went on to his friend Rolleston's place, failed to find him in, returned to his own house, dined and went for a stroll through the streets of the town.

The damage was not so widespread as he had supposed. What is usually described as the first Dieppe earthquake, to distinguish it from the great upheaval of which it was the forerunner, consisted at most of two preliminary oscillations, which were followed forty seconds later by a violent shock accompanied by a tremendous noise and a series of detonations. As for the tidal wave, improperly called an eagre, which rushed up the sea-front, it had but a very moderate height and a quite restricted force. But the people whom Simon met and those with whom he talked remembered those few seconds with a terror which the hours did not appear to diminish. Some were still running with no idea of where they were going, while others—and these were the greater number—remained in a state of absolute stupefaction, making no reply when questioned or answering only with incoherent sentences.

It was of course different in a town like this from elsewhere. In these long-settled regions, where the soil had assumed its irrevocable configuration hundreds and hundreds of years ago and where volcanic manifestations were not even contemplated as possible, any phenomenon of the kind was peculiarly alarming, illogical, abnormal, and in violent contradiction with the laws of nature and with those conditions of security which each of us has the right to regard as unchanging and as definitely fixed by destiny.

And Simon, who since the previous day had been wandering to and fro in this atmosphere of distraction, Simon, who remembered Old Sandstone's unfinished predictions and who had seen the gigantic waterspout in which the *Queen Mary* was swallowed up, Simon asked himself:

"What is happening? What is going to happen? In what unforeseen fashion and by what formidable enemy will the coming attack be delivered?"

Though he had meant to leave Dieppe on that night or the following morning, he felt that his departure would be tantamount to a desertion just when his father was returning and when so many symptoms announced the imminence of a final catastrophe.

"Isabel will advise me," he said to himself. "We will decide together what we have to do."

Meantime night had fallen. He returned to the hotel at nine o'clock and asked that Isabel should be told. He was amazed, almost stunned by the news that Miss Bakefield had gone. She had come down from her room an hour earlier, had handed in at the office a letter addressed to Simon Dubosc and had suddenly left the hotel.

Disconcerted, Simon asked for explanations. There seemed to be none to give, except that one of the waiters said that the young lady had joined a sailor who seemed to be waiting for her in the street and that they had gone off together.

Taking the letter, Simon moved away with the intention of going to a café or entering the hotel, but he had not the courage to wait and it was by the light of a street lamp that he opened the envelope and read:

"I am writing to you with absolute confidence, feeling happy in the certainty that everything I say will be understood and that you will feel neither bitterness nor resentment, nor, after the first painful shock, any real distress.

"Simon, we have made a mistake. It is right that our love, the great and sincere love which we bear each other, should dominate all our thoughts and form the object of our whole lives, but it is not right that this love should be our only rule of conduct and our only obligation. In leaving England we did what is only permissible to those whose fate has persistently thwarted all their dreams and destroyed all their sources of joy. It was an act of liberation and revolt, which people have a right to perform when there is no other alternative than death. But is this the case with us, Simon? What have we done to deserve happiness? What ordeals have we suffered? What efforts have we made? What tears have we shed?

"I have done a great deal of thinking, Simon. I have been thinking of all those poor people who are dead and gone and whose memory will always make me shudder. I have thought of you and myself and my mother. Her too I saw die. You remember: we were speaking of her and of the pearls which she gave me when dying. They are lost; and that distresses me so terribly!

"Simon, I don't want to consider this and still less all the horrors of this awful day as warnings intended for us two. But I do want them to help us to look at life in a different way, to help us put up a prouder and pluckier fight against the obstacles in our path. The fact that you and I are alive while so many others are dead forbids us to suffer in ourselves any sort of weakness, untruth or shuffling, anything that cannot face the broad light of day.

"Win me, Simon. For my part, I shall deserve you by confidence and steadfastness. If we are worthy of each other, we shall succeed and we shall not need to blush for a happiness for which we should now have to pay—as I have felt many times to-day—too high a price of humiliation and shame.

"You will not try to find me, will you, Simon?
"Your promised wife,
"Isabel."

For a few moments Simon stood dumbfounded. As Isabel had foreseen, the first shock was infinitely painful. His mind was full of conflicting ideas which eluded his grasp. He did not attempt to understand nor did he ask himself whether he approved of Isabel's action. He suffered as he had never known that it was possible to suffer.

And suddenly, in the disorder of his mind, among the incoherent suppositions which occurred to him, there flashed a horrible thought. It was obvious that Isabel, determined to submit to her father before the scandal of her flight was noised abroad, had conceived the intention of returning to Lord Bakefield. But how would she put her plan into execution? And Simon remembered that Isabel had left the hotel in the most singular fashion, abruptly, on foot and accompanied by a sailor carrying her bag. Now the landing-stage of the Newhaven steamers was close to the hotel; and the night-boat would cast off her moorings in an hour or two.

"Can she be thinking of crossing?" he muttered, shuddering as he remembered the upheavals of the sea and the wreck of the *Queen Mary*.

He rushed towards the quay. Despite Isabel's expressed wish, he intended to see her; and, if she resisted his love, he would at least implore her to abandon the risk of an immediate crossing.

Directly he reached the quay, he perceived the funnels of the Newhaven steamer behind the harbor railway-station. Isabel, without a doubt, was there, in one of the cabins. There were a good many people about the station and a great deal of piled-up luggage. Simon made for the gangway, but was stopped by an official on duty:

"I have no ticket," said Simon. "I am looking for a lady who has gone on board and who is crossing to-night."

"There are no passengers on board," said the official.

"Really? How's that?"

"The boat is not crossing. There have been orders from Paris. All navigation is suspended."

"Ah!" said Simon Dubosc, with a start of relief. "Navigation is suspended!"

"Yes; that is to say, as far as the line's concerned."

"What do you mean, the line?"

"Why, the company only troubles about its own boats. If others care to put to sea, that is their look-out; we can't prevent them."

"But," said Simon, beginning to feel uneasy, "I suppose none has ventured to sail just lately?"

"Yes, there was one, about an hour ago."

"Oh? Did you see her?"

"Yes, she was a yacht, belonging to an Englishman."

"Edward Rolleston, perhaps?" cried Simon, more or less at a venture.

"Yes, I believe it was, . . . Rolleston. Yes, yes, that's it: an Englishmen who had just put his yacht in commission."

Simon suddenly realized the truth. Rolleston, who was staying at Dieppe, happened to hear of Isabel's arrival, called at her hotel and, at her request, gave orders to sail. Of course, he was the only man capable of risking the adventure and of bribing his crew with a lavish distribution of bank-notes.

The young Englishman's behavior gave proof of such courage and devotion that Simon at once recovered his normal composure. Against Rolleston he felt neither anger nor resentment. He mastered his fears and determined to have confidence.

The clouds were gliding over the town, so low that their black shapes could be distinguished in the darkness of the night. He crossed the front and leant upon the balustrade which borders the

Boulevard Maritime. Thence he could see the white foam of the heavy breakers on the distant sands and hear their vicious assault upon the rocks. Nevertheless, the expected storm was not yet unleashed. More terrible in its continual, nerve-racking menace, it seemed to be waiting for reinforcements and to be delaying its onslaught only to render it more impetuous.

"Isabel will have time to reach the other side," said Simon.

He was now quite calm, full of faith in the present and the future. In absolute agreement with Isabel, he approved of her departure; it caused him no suffering.

"Come," he thought, "it is time to act."

He now recognized the purpose in view of which he had been preparing for years and years: it was to win a woman who was dearer to him than anything on earth and whose conquest would force him to claim that place in the world which his merits deserved.

He had done with hoarding. His duty was to spend, ay, to squander, like a prodigal scattering gold by the handful, without fear of ever exhausting his treasure.

"The time has come," he repeated. "If I am good for anything, I must prove it. If I was right to wait and husband my resources, I must prove it."

He began to walk along the boulevard, his head erect, his chest expanded, striking the ground with a ringing step.

The wind was rising to a gale. Furious showers swept the air. These were trifles to a Simon Dubosc, whose body, clad at all times of the year in light materials, took no heed of the rough weather and, even at the end of a day marked by so many trials, did not betray the slightest symptom of fatigue.

In truth, he felt inaccessible to ordinary weaknesses. His muscles were capable of unlimited endurance. His arms, his legs, his chest, his whole body, patiently exercised, were able to sustain the most violent and persistent efforts. Through his eyes, ears and nostrils he participated acutely in every vibration of the outer world. He was without a flaw. His nerves were perfectly steady. His will responded to every demand. He had the faculty of making up his mind at the first warning. His senses were always on the alert, but were controlled by his reason. He had keen intelligence and a clear, logical mind. *He was ready.*

He was ready. Like an athlete at the top of his form, he owed it to himself to enter the lists and accomplish some feat of prowess. Now, by a wonderful coincidence, it seemed that events promised him a field of action in which this feat of prowess might be performed in the most brilliant fashion. How? That he did not know. When? That he could not say. But he felt a profound intuition that new paths were about to open up before him.

For an hour he walked to and fro, fired by enthusiasm, quivering with hope. Suddenly a squall leapt at the sea-front, as though torn from the crest of the waves; and the rain fell in disorderly masses, hurtling downwards in all directions.

The storm had broken and Isabel was still at sea.

He shrugged his shoulders, refusing to admit a return of anxiety. If they had both escaped from the wreck of the *Queen Mary*, it was not in order that one of them should now pay for that unexpected boon. No, come what might, Isabel would reach the other side. Fate was protecting them both.

Through the torrents of rain pouring across the parade and by the flooded streets, Simon returned to the Villa Dubosc. An indomitable energy bore him up. And he thought with pride of his beautiful bride, who, disdainful like himself of the day's accumulated ordeals and untiring as he, had gone forth bravely into the terrors of the night.

CHAPTER IV

THE GREAT UPHEAVAL

The next five days were of those whose memory oppresses a nation for countless generations. What with hurricanes, cyclones, floods, swollen rivers and tidal waves, the coasts of the Channel and in particular the parts about Fécamp, Dieppe and Le Tréport suffered the most infuriate assaults conceivable.

Although a scientist would not admit the least relation between this series of storms and the tremendous event of the 4th of June, that is to say, of the last of these five days, what a strange coincidence it was! How could the masses ever since help thinking that these several phenomena all formed part of one connected whole?

In Dieppe, the undoubted centre of the first seismic disturbances, in Dieppe and the outlying districts hell was let loose. It was as though this particular spot of the earth's surface was the meeting-place of all the powers that attack and devastate and undermine and slay. In the whirlpools, or the water-spouts, or the eddies of overflowing rivers, under the crash of uprooted trees, crumbling cliffs, falling scaffoldings and walls, tottering belfries and factory-chimneys and of all the objects carried by the wind, the deaths increased steadily. Twenty families were thrown into mourning on the first day, forty on the second. As for the number of victims destroyed by the great convulsion which accompanied the tremendous event, it was doubtful whether this was ever accurately estimated.

As happens in such periods of constant danger, when the individual thinks only of himself and those akin to him, Simon knew hardly anything of the disaster save through the manifestations that reached him directly. After receiving a wireless telegram from Isabel which assured him of her safety, he spread the newspapers only to make certain that his flight with her was not suspected. With the rest—details of the foundering of the *Queen Mary*, articles in which his presence of mind, his courage and Isabel's pluck were extolled, or in which the writer endeavoured to explain the convulsions in the Channel—with all this he had hardly time to concern himself.

He remained with his father. He told him the secret of his love, told him the story of the recent incidents, told him of his plans. Together they wandered through the town or out into the country, both of them drenched and blinded by the showers, staggering under the squalls and bowing their heads beneath the bombardment of slates and tiles. The trees and telegraph-poles along the road were mown down like corn. Trusses of straw, stacks of fodder, faggots of wood, palings, coils of wire were whirled through the air like autumn leaves. Nature seemed to have declared a merciless war upon herself for the sheer pleasure of spoiling and destroying.

And the sea was still trundling its gigantic waves, which broke with deafening roar. All navigation between France and England was suspended. Wireless messages signalled the danger to the great liners coming from America or Germany; and none of them dared enter the hell that was the Channel.

On the fourth day, the last but one, Tuesday the 3rd of June, there was a slight lull.

The final assault was marshalling its forces. M. Dubosc worn out with fatigue, did not get up that afternoon. Simon also threw himself on his bed, fully dressed, and slept until evening. But at nine o'clock a shock awakened them.

Simon thought that the window, which suddenly burst open, had given away under the pressure of the wind. A second shock, more plainly defined, brought down the door of his room; and he felt himself spinning on his own axis, with the walls circling round him.

He ran downstairs and found his father in the garden with the servants, one and all bewildered and uttering incoherent phrases. After a long pause, during which some tried to escape while others were on their knees, there was a violent downpour of rain, mingled with hail, which drove them indoors.

At ten o'clock they sat down to supper. M. Dubosc did not speak a word. The servants were livid and trembling. Simon retained in the depths of his horrified mind an uncanny impression of a shuddering world.

At ten minutes to eleven there was another vibration, of no great violence, but prolonged, with beats that followed one another very closely, like a peal of bells. The china plates fell from the walls; the clock stopped.

All the inmates of the house went out of doors again and crowded into a little thatched summer-house lashed by slanting rain.

Half-an-hour later, the tremors recommenced and from this time onwards, were so to speak, incessant. They were faint and remote at first, but soon grew more and more perceptible, like the shivers of fever which rise from the depths of our flesh and shake us from head to foot.

This ended by becoming a torture. Two of the maids were sobbing. M. Dubosc had flung an arm about Simon's neck and was stammering terrified and meaningless words. Simon himself could no longer endure this execrable sensation of earthquake, this vertigo of the human being losing his foothold. He felt that he was living in a disjointed world and that his mind was registering absurd and grotesque impressions.

From the town arose an uninterrupted clamor. The road was crowded with people fleeing to the heights. A church-bell filled the air with the doleful sound of the tocsin, while the clocks were striking the twelve hours of midnight.

"Let us go away! Let us go away!" cried M. Dubosc.

Simon protested:

"Come, father, there's no need for that! What have we to fear?"

But one and all were seized with panic. Everybody acted at random, making unconscious movements, like a crazy piece of machinery working backwards. The servants went indoors again, looking about them stupidly, as do those who go over a house which they are leaving for the last time. Simon, as in a dream, saw one of them cramming a canvas bag with the gilt candlesticks and silver boxes of which he had charge, while another wrapped himself in a tablecloth and a third filled his pockets with bread and biscuits. He himself, turning by instinct to a small cloak-room on the ground floor, put on a leather jacket and changed his shoes for a pair of heavy shooting-boots. He heard his father saying:

"Here, take my pocket-book. There's money in it, bundles of notes: you'd better have it. . . ."

Suddenly the electric light went out; and at the same time they heard, in the distance, a strange thunder-clap, curiously different from the usual sound of thunder. It was repeated, with a less strident din, accompanied by a subterranean rattling; and then, growing noisier again, it burst a second time in a series of frightful detonations, louder than the roar of artillery.

Then there was a frantic rush for the road. But the fugitives had not left the garden when the frightful catastrophe, announced by so many manifestations, occurred. The earth leapt beneath their feet and instantly fell away and leapt again like an animal in convulsions.

Simon and his father were thrown against each other and then violently torn apart and hurled to the ground. All around them was the stupendous uproar of a tottering world in which everything was collapsing into an incredible chaos. The darkness seemed to have grown denser than ever. And then, suddenly, there was a less distant sound, a sound which touched them, so to speak, a sort of cracking noise. And shrieks rose into the air from the very bowels of the earth.

"Stop!" cried Simon, catching hold of his father, whom he had succeeded in rejoining. "Stop!"

He felt before him, at a distance of a few inches, the utter horror of a gaping abyss; and it was from the bottom of the abyss that the shrieks and howls of their companions rose.

And there were three more shocks. . . .

Simon realized a moment later that his father, clutching his arm, was dragging him away with fierce energy. Both were clambering up the road at a run, groping their way like blind men through the obstacles with which the earthquake had covered it.

M. Dubosc had a goal in view, the Caude-Côte cliff, a bare plateau where they would be in absolute safety. But, on taking a crossroad, they struck against a band of maddened creatures who told them that the cliff had fallen, carrying numerous victims with it. All that these people could think of now was to run to the seashore. With them, M. Dubosc and his son stumbled down the paths which led to the valley of Pourville, whose beach lies in a cove some two miles from Dieppe. The front was obstructed by a crowd of villagers, while others were taking shelter from the rain behind the bathing-huts overturned by the wind. Others again, as the tide was very low, had gone down the sloping shingle and crossed the sands and ventured out to the rocks, as though the danger had ended there and there only. By the uncertain light of a moon which strove to pierce the curtain of the clouds, they could be seen wandering to and fro like ghosts.

"Come, Simon!" said M. Dubosc. "Let's go over there...."

But Simon held him back:

"We are all right here, father. Besides, it seems to be calming down. Take a rest."

"Yes, yes, if you like," replied M. Dubosc, who was in a greatly dejected mood. "And then we will go back to Dieppe. I want to make sure that my boats have not been knocked about too much."

A squall burst, laden with rain.

"Don't move," said Simon. "There's a bathing-hut a few yards off. I'll just go and see...."

He hurried away. But there were already three men lying under the hut, which they had lashed to one of the buttresses of the parade. Others came up and tried to share the shelter. Blows were exchanged. Simon intervened. But the earth shook once more; and they could hear the crash of cliffs falling to right and left.

"Where are you, father?" cried Simon, running back to the spot where he had left M. Dubosc.

Finding no one there, he shouted. But the roar of the gale smothered his voice and he did not know in what direction to seek. Had his father been overcome by fresh fears and gone closer to the sea? Or had he, in his anxiety for his boats, returned to Dieppe as he had hinted?

At a venture—but is it right to apply this term to the unconscious decisions which impel us to follow our destined path?—Simon began to run along the sand and shingle. Then, through the maze of slippery rocks, hampered by the snares spread by the wrack and sea-weed, stumbling into pools of water in which the towering breakers from the open sea had died away in swirling eddies or in lapping waves, he joined the ghostly figures which he had seen from a distance.

He went from one to another and, failing to see his father, was thinking of returning to the parade, when a small incident occurred to make him change his mind. The full moon appeared in the sky. She was covered again immediately, then reappeared; and several times over, between the ragged clouds, her magnificent radiance flooded the sky. At this juncture, Simon, who had veered towards the right of the beach, discovered that the fallen cliffs had buried the shore under the most stupendous chaos imaginable. The white masses were piled one atop the other like so many mountains of chalk. And it looked to Simon as if one of these masses, carried by its own weight, had rolled right into the sea, whence it now rose some three hundred yards away.

On reflection, he could not believe this possible, the distance being far too great; but then what was that enormous shape outstretched yonder like a crouching animal? A hundred times, in his childhood, he had paddled his canoe or come fishing in this part; and he knew for certain that nothing rose above the waters here.

What was it? A sand-bank? But its outlines seemed too uneven and its grey color was that of the rocks, naked rocks, without any covering of wrack or other sea-weed.

He went forward, actuated in part by an eager curiosity, but still more by some mysterious and all-powerful force, the spirit of adventure. The adventure appealed to him: he must go up to this new ground whose origin he could not help attributing to the recent earthquake.

And he went up to it. Beyond the first belt of sand, beyond the belt of small rocks where he stood, was the final bed of sand over which the waves rolled eternally. But from place to place there rose still more rocks, so that he was able, by a persistent effort, to reach what appeared to be a sort of promontory.

The ground underfoot was hard, consisting of sedimentary deposits, as Old Sandstone would have said. And Simon realized that, as a result of the violent shocks and of some physical phenomenon whose action he did not understand, the bed of the sea had been forced upwards until it overtopped the waves by a height which varied in different places, but which certainly exceeded the level of the highest spring tides.

The promontory was of no great width, for by the intermittent light of the moon Simon could see the foam of the breakers leaping on either side of this new reef. It was irregular in form, thirty or forty yards wide in one part and a hundred or even two hundred in another; and it ran on like a continuous embankment, following more or less closely the old line of the cliffs.

Simon did not hesitate. He set out. The hilly, uneven surface, at first interspersed with pools of water and bristling with rocks which the stubborn labors of the sea had pushed thus far, became gradually flatter; and Simon was able to walk at a fair pace, though hampered by a multitude of objects, often half-buried in the ground, which the waves, not affecting the bottom of the sea, had been unable to sweep away: meat-tins, old buckets, scrap-iron, shapeless utensils of all kinds covered with sea-weed and encrusted with little shells.

A few minutes later, he perceived Dieppe lying on his right, a scene of desolation which he divined rather than saw. The light of conflagrations not wholly extinguished reddened the sky; and the town looked to him like an unhappy city in which a horde of barbarians had sat encamped for weeks on end. The earth had merely shuddered and an even more stupendous disaster had ensued.

At this moment, a fine tracery of grey clouds spread above the great black banks which were driving before the gale; and the moon disappeared. Simon felt irresolute. Since all the light-houses were demolished, how would he find his way if the darkness increased? He thought of his father, who was perhaps anxious, but he thought also—and more ardently—of his distant bride whom he had to win; and, as the idea of this conquest was blended in his mind—he could not have said why—with visions of dangers accepted and with extraordinary happenings, he felt vaguely that he would be right in going on. To go on meant travelling towards something formidable and unknown. The soil which had risen from the depths might sink again. The waves might reconqueror the lost ground and cut off all retreat. An unfathomable gulf might yawn beneath his footsteps. To go on was madness.

And he went on.

CHAPTER V

VIRGIN SOIL

It was hardly later than one o'clock in the morning. The storm was less furious and the squalls had ceased, so that Simon suddenly began to walk as quickly as the trifling obstacles over which he stumbled and the dim light of the sky would permit. For that matter, if he branched off too far in either direction, the nearer sound of the waves would serve as a warning.

In this way he passed Dieppe and followed a direction which, while it varied by reason of curves and sudden turns, nevertheless, in his opinion, ran parallel with the Norman coast. During the whole of this first stage of his journey, he was only half-aware of what he was doing and had no thought but of making headway, feeling certain that his explorations would be interrupted from one minute to the next. It did not seem to him that he was penetrating into unlimited regions, but rather that he was really persistently pushing towards a goal which was close at hand, but which receded so soon as he approached it and which was no other than the extreme point of this miraculous peninsula.

"There," he said to himself. "There it is. I've got there. The new ground goes as far as that. . . ."

But the new ground continued to stretch into the darkness; and a little later he repeated:

"It's over there. The line of breakers is closing up. I can see it."

But the line opened out, leaving a passage by which Simon pursued his way.

Two o'clock. . . . Half-past two. . . . Sometimes the water was up to his knees, sometimes his feet sank into a bed of thicker sand. These were the low-lying parts, the valleys of the peninsula; and there might perhaps be some, thought Simon where these beds would be deep enough to bar his passage. He went on all the more briskly. Ascents rose in front of him, leading him to mounds forty or fifty feet in height, whose farther slopes he descended rapidly. And, lost in the immensity of the sea, imprisoned by it, absorbed by it, he had the illusion that he was running over its surface, along the back of great frozen, motionless waves.

He halted. Before him a speck of light had crossed the darkness, a long, a very long way off. Four times he saw the flame reappear at regular intervals. Fifteen seconds later came a fresh series of flashes, followed by a similar interval of darkness.

"A light-house!" murmured Simon. "A light-house which the disaster has spared!"

Just here the embankment ran in the direction of the light-house; and Simon calculated that it would thus end at Tréport, or perhaps farther north, if the light-house marked the estuary of the Somme, which was highly probable. In that case he would have to walk four or five hours longer, at the same swift pace.

But he lost the intermittent gleams as suddenly as he had caught sight of them. He looked and failed to find them and felt overwhelmed, as though, after the death of these little twinkling flames, he could no longer hope ever to escape from the heavy darkness which was stifling him or to discover the tremendous secret in pursuit of which he had darted. What was he doing? Where was he? What did it all mean? What was the use of making such efforts?

"Forward!" he cried. "At the double! and we don't do any more thinking. I shall understand presently, when I get there. Until then, it's a matter of going on and on, like a beast of burden."

He spoke aloud, to shake off his drowsiness. And, as a protest against a weakness of which he was ashamed, he set off at a run.

It was a quarter past three. In the keener air of the morning he was conscious of a sense of well-being. Moreover, he noticed that the obscurity around him was becoming lighter and was gradually lifting like a mist.

The first glimmer of dawn appeared. The day broke quickly and at last the new land was visible to Simon's eyes, grey, as he had supposed, and yellower in places, with streaks of sand and hollows filled with water in which all sorts of fish were seen struggling or dying, with a whole galaxy of little islands and irregular shoals, beaches of fine, close-packed gravel, tracts of sea-weed and gentle undulations, like those of a rich plain.

And in the midst of it all there was ever a multitude of objects whose real shape could no longer be distinguished, remnants enlarged and swollen by the addition of everything that could be encrusted or fastened on them, or else eaten away, worn out, corroded, or disintegrated by everything that helps to dissolve or to destroy.

They were flotsam and jetsam of all kinds. Past counting, glistening with slime, of all types and of all materials, of an age to be reckoned in months or years, it might be in centuries, they bore witness to the unbroken procession of thousands and thousands of wrecks. And, as many as were these remnants of wood and iron, so many were the human lives engulfed in companies of tens and hundreds. Youth, health, wealth, hope: each wreck represented the destruction of all their dreams, of all their realities; and each also recalled the distress of the living, the mourning of mothers and wives.

And the field of death stretched away indefinitely, an immense, tragic cemetery, such as the earth had never known, with endless lines of graves, tombstones and funeral monuments. To the right and left there was nothing, nothing but a dense fog rising from the water, hiding the horizon as completely as the veils of night and making it impossible for Simon to see more than a hundred yards in front of him. But from this fog new land-formations continued to emerge; and this seemed to him to fall so strictly within the domain of the fabulous and the incredible that he easily imagined them to be rising from the depths on his approach and assuming form and substance to offer him a passage.

A little after four o'clock there was a return of the gale, an offensive of ugly clouds emitting volleys of rain and hail. The wind made a gap in the clouds, which it drove north and south, and then, on Simon's right, parallel with a belt of rosy light which divided the waves from the black sky, the coast-line became visible.

It was a vaguely defined line which might have been taken for a fine streak of motionless clouds; but he knew its general appearance so well that he did not hesitate for a moment. It was the cliffs of the Seine-Inférieurs and the Somme, between Le Tréport and Cayeux.

He rested for a few minutes; then, to lighten his outfit, he pulled off his boots, which were too heavy, and his leather jacket, which was making him too hot. Then taking his father's wallet out of the jacket, he found in one of the pockets two biscuits and a stick of chocolate which he himself had put there, so to speak, unwittingly.

After making a meal of these, he set out again briskly, not with the cautious gait of an explorer who does not know whither he is going and who measures his efforts, but at the pace of an athlete who has fixed his time-table and keeps to it in spite of obstacles and difficulties. A strange light-heartedness uplifted him. He was glad to expend so much of the force which he had been storing for all these years and to expend it on a task of which he knew nothing, but of which he felt the exceptional greatness. His elbows were well tucked in and his head thrown back. His bare feet marked the sand with a faint trail. The wind bathed his face and played in and out of his hair. What joy!

He kept up his pace for nearly four hours. Why should he hold himself in? He was always expecting the new formation to change its direction and, bending suddenly to the right, to join the coast of the Somme. And he went forward in all confidence.

At certain points, progress became arduous. The sea had got up; and here and there the waves, rushing over those places where the sand, though clear of the water, was unprotected by a barrier of rocks, formed in the narrower portions actual rivers, flowing from one side to the other, which Simon had to wade, almost knee-deep in water. Moreover, he had taken so little food that he began to be racked with hunger. He had to slow down. And another hour went by.

The great squalls had blown over. The returning sea-fogs seemed to have deadened the wind and were now closing in on him again. Once more Simon was walking through moving clouds which concealed his path from him. Less sure of himself, attacked by a sudden sense of loneliness and distress, he soon experienced a lassitude to which he was unwilling to surrender.

This was a mistake. He recognized the fact: nevertheless, he struggled on as though in fulfillment of the most imperious duty. With an obstinate ring in his voice, he gave himself his orders:

"Forward: Ten minutes more! . . . You must! . . . And, once more, ten minutes!"

On either side lay things which, in any other circumstances, would have held his attention. An iron chest, three old guns, small-arms, cannon-balls, a submarine. Enormous fish lay stranded on the sand. Sometimes a white sea-gull circled through space.

And so he came to a great wreck whose state of preservation betrayed a recent disaster. It was an overturned steamer, with her keel deeply buried in a sandy hollow, while her black stern stood erect, displaying a broad pink stripe on which Simon read:

"The *Bonne Vierge.* Calais."

And he remembered. The *Bonne Vierge* was one of the two boats whose loss had been announced in the telegrams posted up at Newhaven. Employed in the coasting-trade between the north and west of France, she had sunk at a spot which lay in a direct line between Calais and Le Havre; and Simon saw in this a positive proof that he was still following the French coast, passing those seamarks whose names he now recalled: the Ridin de Dieppe, the Bassure de Baas, the Vergoyer and so on.

It was ten o'clock in the morning. From the average pace which he had maintained, allowing for deviation and for hilly ground, Simon calculated that he had covered a distance of nearly forty miles as the crow flies and that he ought to find himself approximately on a level with Le Touquet.

"What am I risking if I push on?" he asked himself. "At most I should have to do another forty miles to pass through the Straits of Dover and come out into the North Sea . . . in which case my position would be none too cheerful. But it will be devilish odd if, between this and that, I don't touch land somewhere. The only trouble is, whether it's forty miles on or forty miles back, those things can't be done on an empty stomach."

Fortunately, for he was feeling symptoms of a fatigue to which he was unaccustomed, the problem solved itself without his assistance. After going round the wreck, he managed to crawl under the poop and there discovered a heap of packing-cases which evidently formed part of the cargo. All were more or less split or broken or gaping at the corners. But one of them, whose lid Simon had no difficulty in prying open, contained tins of syrup, bottles of wine and stacks of canned foods: meat, fish, vegetables and fruits.

"Splendid!" he said, laughing. "Luncheon is served, sir. On top of that, a little rest; and the sooner I'm off the better!"

He made an excellent lunch; and a long siesta, under the vessel, among the packing-cases, restored his strength completely. When he woke and saw that his watch was already pointing to noon, he felt uneasy at the waste of time and suddenly reflected that others must have taken the same path and would now be able to catch him up and outstrip him. And he did not intend this to happen. Accordingly, feeling as fit as at the moment of starting, provided with the indispensable provisions and determined to follow up the adventure to the very end, without a companion to share his glory or to rob him of it, he set off again at a very brisk, unflagging pace.

"I shall get there," he thought, "I mean to get there. All this is an unprecedented phenomenon, the creation of a tract of land which will utterly change the conditions of life in this part of the world. I mean to be there first and to see . . . to see what? I don't know, *but I mean to do it.*"

What rapture to tread a soil on which no one has ever set foot! Men travel in search of this rapture to the utmost ends of the earth, to remote countries, no matter where; and very often the secret is hardly worth discovering. As for Simon, he was having his wonderful adventure in the heart of the oldest regions of old Europe. The Channel! The French coast! To be treading virgin soil here, of all places, where mankind had lived for three or four thousand years! To behold sights that no other eye had ever looked upon! To come after the Gauls, the Romans, the Franks, the Anglo-Saxons and to be the first to pass! To be the first to pass this way, ahead of the millions and millions of men who would follow in his track, on the new path which he would have inaugurated!

One o'clock. . . . Half-past one. . . . More ridges of sand, more wrecks. Always that curtain of clouds. And always Simon's lingering impression of a goal which eluded him. The tide, still low, was leaving a greater number of islands uncovered. The waves were breaking far out to sea and rolling across wide sand-banks as though the new land had widened considerably.

About two o'clock in the afternoon, he came upon higher undulations followed by a series of sandy flats in which his feet sank to a greater depth than usual. Absorbed by the dreary spectacle of a ship's mast protruding from the sand, with its tattered and colored flag flopping in the wind, he pressed on all unsuspecting. In a few minutes, the sand was up to his knees, then half-way up his thighs. He laughed, still unheeding.

In the end, however, unable to advance, he tried to return: his efforts were useless. He attempted to lift his legs by treading, as though climbing a flight of stairs, but he could not. He brought his hands into play, laying them flat on the sands: they too went under.

Then he broke into a flood of perspiration. He suddenly understood the hideous truth: he was caught in a quicksand.

It was soon over. He did not sink with the slowness that lends a little hope to the agony of despair. Simon fell, so to speak, into a void. His hips, his waist, his chest disappeared. His outstretched arms checked his descent for a moment. He stiffened his body, he struggled. In vain. The sand rose like water to his shoulders, to his neck.

He began to shout. But in the immensity of these solitudes, to whom was his appeal addressed? Nothing could save him from the most horrible of deaths. Then it was that he shut his eyes and with clenched lips sealed his mouth, which was already full of the taste of the sand, and, in a fit of terror, he gave himself up for lost.

CHAPTER VI

TRIUMPH

Afterwards, he never quite understood the chance to which he owed his life. The most that he could remember was that one of his feet touched something solid which served him as a support and that something else enabled him to advance, now a step, now two or three, to lift himself little by little out of his living tomb and to leave it alive. What had happened? Had he come upon a loose plank of the buried vessel whose flag he saw before him? He did not know. But what he never forgot was the horror of that minute, which was followed by such a collapse of all his will and strength that he remained for a long time lying on a piece of wreckage, unable to move a limb and shuddering all over with fever and mental anguish.

He set off again mechanically, under the irresistible influence of confused feelings which bade him go forward and reconnoitre. But he had lost his former energy. His eyes remain obstinately fixed upon the ground. For no appreciable reason, he judged certain spots to be dangerous and avoided them by making a circuit, or even leapt back as though at the sight of an abyss. Simon Dubosc was afraid.

Moreover, after reading on a piece of wood from a wreck the name of Le Havre, that is to say, the port which lay behind him, he asked himself anxiously whether the new land had not changed its direction; whether, by doubling upon itself, it was not leading him into the widest part of the Channel.

The thought of no longer knowing where he was or whither he was going increased his lassitude twofold. He felt overwhelmed, discouraged, terribly alone. He had no hope of rescue, either by sea, on which no boat would dare put out, or from the air, which the sea-fog had made impossible for aeroplanes. What would happen then?

Nevertheless he walked on; and the hours went by; and the belt of land unrolled vaguely before his eyes the same monotonous spectacle, the same melancholy sand-hills, the same dreary landscapes on which no sun had ever shone.

"I shall get there," he repeated, stubbornly. "I mean to get there; I must and shall."

Four o'clock. He often looked at his watch, as though expecting a miraculous intervention at some precise moment, he did not know when. Worn out by excessive and ill-directed efforts, exhausted by the fear of a hideous death, he was gradually yielding beneath the weight of a fatigue which tortured his body and unhinged his brain. He was afraid. He dreaded the trap laid for him by the sands. He dreaded the threatening night, the storm and, above all, hunger, for all his provisions had been lost in the abyss of the quicksand.

The agony which he suffered! A score of times he was on the point of stretching himself on the ground and abandoning the struggle. But the thought of Isabel sustained him; and he walked on and on.

And then, suddenly, an astonishing sight held him motionless. Was it possible? He hesitated to believe it, so incredible did the reality seem to him. But how could he doubt the evidence of his eyes?

He stooped forward. Yes, it was really that: there were footprints! The ground was marked with footprints, the prints of two bare feet, very plainly defined and apparently quite recent.

And immediately his stupefaction made way for a great joy, aroused by the sudden and clear conception of a most undeniable fact: the new land was indeed connected, as he had supposed, with some point on the northern coast of France; and from this point, which could not be very remote, in view of the distance which he himself had covered, one of his fellow-creatures had come thus far.

Delighted to feel that there was human life near at hand, he recollected the incident where Robinson Crusoe discovers the imprint of a naked foot on the sand of his desert island:

"It's Man Friday's footprint!" he said, laughing. "There is a Friday, too, in this land of mine! Let's see if we can find him!"

At the point where he had crossed the trail, it branched off to the left and approached the sea. Simon was feeling surprised at not meeting or catching sight of any one, when he discovered that the author of the footprints, after going round a shapeless wreck, had turned and was therefore walking in the same direction as himself.

After twenty minutes, the trail, intersected by a gully which ran across it, escaped him for a time. He found it again and followed it, skirting the base of a chain of rather high sand-hills, which ended suddenly in a sort of craggy cliff.

On rounding this cliff Simon started back. On the ground, flat on its face, with the arms at right angles to the body, lay the corpse of a man, curiously dressed in a very short, yellow leather waistcoat and a pair of trousers, likewise leather, the ends of which were bell-shaped and slit in the Mexican fashion. In the middle of his back was the hilt of a dagger which had been driven between the shoulder-blades.

What astonished Simon when he had turned the body over was that the face was brick-red, with prominent cheek-bones and long, black hair: it was the undoubted face of a Redskin. Blood trickled from the mouth, which was distorted by a hideous grin. The eyes were wide open, and showed only their whites. The contracted fingers had gripped the sand like claws. The body was still warm.

"It can't be an hour since he was killed," said Simon, whose hand was trembling. And he added, "What the deuce brought the fellow here? By what unheard-of chance have I come upon a Redskin in this desert?"

The dead man's pockets contained no papers to give Simon any information. But, near the body, within the actual space in which the struggle had taken place, another trail of footsteps came to an end, a double trail, made by the patterned rubber soles of a man who had come and gone. And, ten yards away, Simon picked up a gold hundred-franc piece, with the head of Napoleon I. and the date 1807.

He followed this double trail, which led him to the edge of the sea. Here a boat had been put aground. It was now easy to reconstruct the tragedy. Two men who had landed on this newly-created shore had set out to explore it, each taking his own direction. One of them, an Indian, had found, in the hulk of some wreck, a certain quantity of gold coins, perhaps locked up in a strong-box. The other, to obtain the treasure for himself, had murdered his companion, and reëmbarked.

Thus, on this virgin soil, Simon was confronted—it was the first sign of life—with a crime, with an act of treachery, with armed cupidity committing murder, with the human animal. A man finds gold. One of his fellows attacks and kills him.

Simon pushed onwards without further delay, feeling certain that these two men, doubtless bolder than the rest, were only the forerunners of others coming from the mainland. He was eager to see these others, to question them upon the point whence they had started, the distance which they had covered and many further particulars which as yet remained unexplained.

The thought of this meeting filled him with such happiness that he resisted his longing for rest. Yet what a torture was this almost uninterrupted effort! He had walked for sixteen hours since leaving Dieppe. It was eighteen hours since the moment when the great upheaval had driven him from his home. In ordinary times the effort would not have been beyond his strength. But under what lamentable conditions had he accomplished it!

He walked on and on. Rest? And what if the others, coming behind him from Dieppe, should succeed in catching him up?

The scene was always the same. Wrecks marked his path, like so many tomb-stones. The mist still hung above the endless grave-yard.

After walking an hour, he was brought to a stop. The sea barred his way.

The sea facing him! His disappointment was not unmixed with anger. Was this then the limit of his journey and were all these convulsions of nature to end merely in the creation of a peninsula cut off in this meaningless fashion?

But, on scanning from the sloping shore the waves tossing their foam to where he stood, he perceived at some distance a darker mass, which gradually emerged from the mist; and he felt sure that this was a continuation of the newly-created land, beyond a depression covered by the sea:

"I must get across," said Simon.

He removed his clothes, made them into a bundle, tied it round his neck and entered the water. For him the crossing of this strait, in which, besides, he was for some time able to touch bottom, was mere child's-play. He landed, dried himself and resumed his clothes.

A very gentle ascent led him, after some five hundred yards, to a reef, overtopped by actual hills of sand, but of sand so firm that he did not hesitate to set foot on it. He therefore climbed till he reached the highest crest of these hills.

And it was here, at this spot—where a granite column was raised subsequently, with an inscription in letters of gold: two names and a date—it was here, on the 4th of June, at ten minutes past six in the evening, above a vast amphitheatre girt about with sand-hills like the benches of a circus, it was here that Simon Dubosc at last saw, climbing to meet him, a man.

He did not move at first, so strong was his emotion. The man came on slowly, sauntering, as it were, examining his surroundings and picking his way. When at last he raised his head, he gave a start of surprise at seeing Simon and then waved his cap. Then Simon rushed towards him, with outstretched arms and an immense longing to press him to his breast.

At a distance the stranger seemed a young man. He was dressed like a fisherman, in a brown canvas smock and trousers. His feet were bare; he was tall and broad-shouldered. Simon shouted to him:

"I've come from Dieppe. You, what town do you come from? Did you take long to get here? Are you alone?"

He could see that the fisherman was smiling and that his tanned, clean-shaven face wore a frank and happy expression.

They met and clasped hands; and Simon repeated:

"I started from Dieppe at one in the morning. And you? What port do you come from?"

The man began to laugh and replied in words which Simon could not understand. He did not understand them, though he well enough recognized the language in which they were uttered. It was English, but a dialect spoken by the lower orders. He concluded that this was an English fisherman employed at Calais or Dunkirk.

He spoke to him again, dwelling on his syllables and pointing to the horizon:

"Calais? Dunkirk?"

The other repeated these two names as well as he could, as though trying to grasp their meaning. At last his face lit up and he shook his head.

Then, turning round and pointing in the direction from which he had come, he twice said:

"Hastings. . . . Hastings. . . ."

Simon started. But the amazing truth did not appear to him at once, though he was conscious of its approach and was absolutely dumbfounded. Of course, the fisherman was referring to Hastings as his birthplace or his usual home. But where had he come from at this moment?

Simon made a suggestion:

"Boulogne? Wimereux?"

"No, no!" replied the stranger. "Hastings. . . . England. . . ."

And his arm pointed persistently to the same quarter of the horizon, while he as persistently repeated:

"England. . . . England. . . ."

"What? What's that you're saying?" cried Simon. And he seized the man violently by the shoulders. "What's that you're saying? That's England behind you? You've come from England? No, no! You can't mean that. It's not true!"

The sailor struck the ground with his foot:

"*England!*" he repeated, thus denoting that the ground which he had stamped upon led to the English mainland.

Simon was flabbergasted. He took out his watch and moved his forefinger several times round the dial.

"What time did you start? How many hours have you been walking?"

"Three," replied the Englishman, opening his fingers.

"Three hours!" muttered Simon. "We are three hours from the English coast!"

This time the whole stupendous truth forced itself upon him. At the same moment he realized what had caused his mistake. As the French coast ran due north, from the estuary of the Somme, it was inevitable that, in pursuing a direction parallel to the French coast, he should end by reaching the English coast at Folkestone or Dover, or, if his path inclined slightly toward the west, at Hastings.

Now he had not taken this into account. Having had proof on three occasions that France was on his right and not behind him, he had walked with his mind dominated by the certainty that France was close at hand and that her coast might loom out of the fog at any moment.

And it was the English coast! And the man who had loomed into sight was a man of England!

What a miracle! How his every nerve throbbed as he held this man in his arms and gazed into his friendly face! He was exalted by the intuition of the extraordinary things which the tremendous event of the last few hours implied, in the present and the future; and his meeting with this man of England was the very symbol of that event.

And the fisherman, too, felt the incomparable grandeur of the moment which had brought them together. His quiet smile was full of solemnity. He nodded his head in silence. And the two men, face to face, looking into each other's eyes, gazed at each other with the peculiar affection of those who have never been parted, who have striven side by side and who receive together the reward of their actions performed in common.

The Englishman wrote his name on a piece of paper: William Brown. And Simon, yielding to one of his natural outbursts of enthusiasm, said:

"William Brown, we do not speak the same language; you do not understand me and I understand you only imperfectly; and still we are bound together more closely than two loving brothers could be. Our embrace has a significance which we cannot yet imagine. You and I represent the two greatest and noblest countries in the world; and they are mingled together in our two persons."

He was weeping. The Englishman still smiled, but his eyes were moist with tears. Excitement, excessive fatigue, the violence of the emotions which he had experienced that day, produced in Simon a sort of intoxication in which he found an unsuspected source of energy.

"Come," he said to the fisherman catching hold of his arm. "Come, show me the way."

He would not even allow William Brown to help him in difficult places, so determined was he to accomplish this glorious and magnificent undertaking by his unaided efforts.

This last stage of his journey lasted three hours.

Almost at the start they passed three Englishmen, to whom Brown addressed a few words and who, while continuing on their road, uttered exclamations of surprise. Then came two more, who stopped for a moment while Brown explained the situation. These two turned back with Simon and the fisherman; and all four, on coming closer to the sea, were attracted by a voice appealing for help.

Simon ran forward and was the first to reach a woman lying on the sand. The waves were drenching her with their spray. She was bound by cords which fettered her legs, held her arms motionless against her body, pressed the wet silk of her blouse against her breast and bruised the bare flesh of her shoulders. Her black hair, cut rather short and fastened in front by a little gold chain, framed a dazzling face, with lips like the petals of a red flower and a warm, brown skin, burnt by the sun. The face, to an artist like Simon, was of a brilliant beauty and recalled to his mind certain feminine types which he had encountered in Spain or South America. Quickly he cut her bonds; and then, as his companions were approaching before he had time to question her, he slipped off his jacket and covered her beautiful shoulders with it.

She gave him a grateful glance, as though this delicate act was the most precious compliment which he could pay her:

"Thank you, thank you!" she murmured. "You are French, are you not?"

But groups of people came hurrying along, followed by a more numerous company. Brown told the story of Simon's adventure; and Simon found himself separated from the young woman without learning more about her. People crowded about him, asking him questions. At every moment fresh crowds mingled with the procession which bore him along in its midst.

All these people seemed to Simon unusually excited and strange in their behavior. He soon learnt that the earthquake had devastated the English coast. Hastings, having been, like Dieppe, a centre of seismic shocks, was partly destroyed.

About eight o'clock they came to the edge of a deep depression quite two-thirds of a mile in width. Filled with water until the middle of the afternoon, this depression, by a stroke of luck for Simon, had delayed the progress of those who were flying from Hastings and who had ventured upon the new land.

A few minutes later, the fog being now less dense, Simon was able to distinguish the endless row of houses and hotels which lines the sea-fronts of Hastings and St. Leonards. By this time, his escort consisted of three or four hundred people; and many others, doubtless driven from their houses, were wandering in all directions with dazed expressions on their faces.

The throng about him became so thick that soon he was able to see nothing in the heavy gloom of the twilight but their crowded heads and shoulders. He replied as best he could to the thousand questions which were put to him; and his replies, repeated from mouth to mouth, aroused cries of astonishment and admiration.

Gradually, lights appeared in the Hastings windows. Simon, exhausted but indomitable, was walking briskly, sustained by a nervous energy which seemed to be renewed as and when he expended it. And suddenly he burst out laughing to think—and certainly no thought could have been more stimulating or better calculated to give a last fillip to his failing strength—to think that he, Simon Dubosc, a man of the good old Norman stock, was setting foot in England at the very spot where William the Conqueror, Duke of Normandy, had landed in the eleventh century! Hastings! King Harold and his mistress, Edith of the swan's neck! The great adventure of yore was being reënacted! For the second time the virgin isle was conquered . . . and conquered by a Norman!

"I believe destiny is favoring me, my Lord Bakefield," he said to himself.

The new land joined the mainland between Hastings and St. Leonards. It was intersected by valleys and fissures, bristling with rocks and fragments of the cliffs, in the midst of which lay, in an indescribable jumble, the wreckage of demolished piers, fallen lighthouses, stranded and shattered ships. But Simon saw nothing of all this. His eyes were too weary to distinguish things save through a mist.

They reached the shore. What happened next? He was vaguely conscious that some one was leading him, through streets with broken pavements and between heaps of ruins, to the hall of a casino, a strange, dilapidated building, with tottering walls and a gaping roof, but nevertheless radiant with electric light.

The municipal authorities had assembled here to receive him. Champagne was drunk. Hymns of rejoicing were sung with religious fervour. A stirring spectacle and, at the same time, a striking proof of the national self-control, this celebration improvised in the midst of a town in ruins. But every one present had the impression that something of a very great importance had occurred, something so great that it outweighed the horror of the catastrophe and the consequent mourning: France and England were united!

France and England were united; and the first man who had walked from the one country to the other by the path which had risen from the very depths of the ancient Channel that used to divide them was there, in their midst. What could they do but honor him? He represented in his magnificent effort the vitality and the inexhaustible ardor of France. He was the hero and the herald of the most mysterious future.

A tremendous burst of cheering rose to the platform on which he stood. The crowd thronged about him, the men shook him by the hand, the ladies kissed him. They pressed him to make a speech which all could hear and understand. And Simon, leaning over these people, whose enthusiasm blended with his own exaltation, stammered a few words in praise of the two nations.

The frenzy was so violent and unbridled that Simon was jostled, carried off his feet, swept into the crowd and lost among the very people who were looking for him. His only thought was to go into the first hotel that offered and throw himself down on a bed. A hand seized his; and a voice said:

"Come with me; I will show you the way."

He recognized the young woman whom he had released from her bonds. Her face likewise was transfigured with emotion.

"You have done a splendid thing," she said. "I don't believe any other man could have done it. . . . You are above all other men. . . ."

An eddy in the crowd tore them apart, although the stranger's hand clutched his. He fell to the floor among the overturned chairs, picked himself up again and was feeling at the end of his tether as he neared one of the exits, when suddenly he stood to attention. Strength returned to his limbs. Lord Bakefield and Isabel were standing before him.

Eagerly Isabel held out her hand:

"We were there, Simon. We saw you. I'm proud of you, Simon."

He was astonished and confused.

"Isabel! Is it really you?"

She smiled, happy to see him so much moved in her presence.

"It really is; and it's quite natural, since we live at Battle, a mile away. The catastrophe has spared the house but we came to Hastings to help the sufferers and in that way heard of your arrival . . . of your triumph, Simon."

Lord Bakefield did not budge. He pretended to be looking in another direction. Simon addressed him.

"May I take it, Lord Bakefield, that you will regard this day's work as a first step towards the goal for which I am making?"

The old nobleman, stiff with pride and resentment, vouchsafed no reply.

"Of course," Simon continued, "I haven't conquered England. But all the same there seem to be a series of circumstances in my favor which permit me at least to ask you whether you consider that the first of your conditions has been fulfilled."

This time Lord Bakefield seemed to be making up his mind. But, just as he was going to reply—and his features expressed no great amount of good-will—Isabel intervened:

"Don't ask my father any questions, Simon . . . He appreciates the wonderful thing that you have done at its true value. But you and I have offended him too seriously for him to be able to forgive you just yet. We must let time wipe out the unpleasant memory."

"Time!" echoed Simon, with a laugh. "Time! The trouble is that I have only twelve days left in which to triumph over all the labors put upon me. After conquering England, I have still to win the laurels of Hercules . . . or of Don Quixote."

"Well," she said, "in the meantime hurry off and go to bed. That's the best thing you can do for the moment."

And she drew Lord Bakefield away with her.

CHAPTER VII

LYNX-EYE

"What do you say to this, my boy? Did I prophesy it all, or did I not? Read my pamphlet on *The Channel in the Year 2000* and you'll see. And then remember all I told you the other morning, at Newhaven station. Well, there you are: the two countries are joined together as they were once before, in the Eocene epoch."

Awakened with a start by Old Sandstone, Simon, with eyes still heavy with slumber, gazed vacantly at the hotel bed-room in which he had been sleeping, at his old professor, walking to and fro, and at another person, who was sitting in the dark and who seemed to be an acquaintance of Old Sandstone's.

"Ah!" yawned Simon. "But what's the time?"

"Seven o'clock in the evening, my son."

"What? Seven o'clock? Have I been sleeping since last night's meeting at the Casino?"

"Rather! I was strolling about this morning, when I heard of your adventure. 'Simon Dubosc! I know him.' said I. I ran like mad. I rapped on the door. I came in. Nothing would wake you. I went away, came back again and so on, until I decided to sit down by your bedside and wait."

Simon leapt out of bed. New clothes and clean linen had been laid out in the bathroom; and he saw, hanging on the wall, his jacket, the same with which he had covered the bare shoulders of the young woman whom he had released.

"Who brought that?" he asked.

"That? What?" asked Old Sandstone.

Simon turned to him.

"Tell me, professor, did any one come to this room while you were here?"

"Yes, lots of people. They came in as they liked: admirers, idle sightseers. . . ."

"Did a woman come in?"

"Upon my word, I didn't notice.... Why?"

"Why?" replied Simon, explaining. "Because last night, while I was asleep, I several times had the impression that a woman came up to me and bent over me...."

Old Sandstone shrugged his shoulders:

"You've been dreaming, my boy. When one's badly overtired, one's likely to have those nightmares...."

"But it wasn't in the very least a nightmare!" said Simon, laughing.

"It's stuff and nonsense, in any case!" cried Old Sandstone. "What does it matter? There's only one thing that matters: this sudden joining up of the two coasts . . . ! It's fairly tremendous, what? What do you think of it? It's more than a bridge thrown from shore to shore. It's more than a tunnel. It's a flesh-and-blood tie, a permanent junction, an isthmus, what? The Sussex Isthmus, the Isthmus of Normandy, they've already christened it."

Simon jested:

"Oh, an isthmus! ... A mere causeway, at most!"

"You're drivelling!" cried Old Sandstone. "Don't you know what happened last night? Why, of course not, the fellow knows nothing! He was asleep! ... Then you didn't realize that there was another earthquake? Quite a slight one, but still . . . an earthquake? No? You didn't wake up? In that case, my boy, listen to the incredible truth, which surpasses what any one could have foreseen. It's no longer a question of the strip of earth which you crossed from Dieppe to Hastings. That was the first attempt, just a little trial phenomenon. But since then . . . oh, since then, my boy . . . you're listening, aren't you? Well, there, from Fécamp to Cape Gris-nez in France and from the west of Brighton to Folkestone in England: all that part, my boy, is now one solid mass. Yes, it forms a permanent junction, seventy to ninety miles wide, a bit of exposed ground equivalent at least to two large French departments or two fair-sized English counties. Nature hasn't done badly . . . for a few hours' work! What say you?"

Simon listened in amazement:

"Is it possible? Are you sure? But then it will be the cause of unspeakable losses. Think: all the coast-towns ruined ... and trade ... navigation...."

And Simon, thinking of his father and the vessels locked up in Dieppe harbor, repeated:

"Are you quite sure?"

"Why, of course I am!" said Old Sandstone, to whom all these considerations were utterly devoid of interest. "Of course I'm sure! A hundred telegrams, from all sides, vouch for the fact. What's more, read the evening papers. Oh, I give you my word, it's a blessed revolution! . . . The earthquake? The victims? We hardly mention them! . . . Your Franco-English raid? An old story! No, there's only one thing that matters to-day, on this side of the Channel: England is no longer an Island; she forms part of the European continent; she is riveted on to France!"

"This," said Simon, "is one of the greatest facts in history!"

"It's *the* greatest, my son. Since the world has been a world and since men have been gathered into nations, there has been no physical phenomenon of greater importance than this. And to think that I predicted the whole thing, the causes and the effects, the causes which I am the only one to know!"

"And what are they?" asked Simon. "How is it that I was able to pass? How is it. . . ."

Old Sandstone checked him with a gesture which reminded Simon of the way in which his former lecturer used to begin his explanations at college; and the old codger, taking a pen and a sheet of paper, proceeded:

"Do you know what a fault is? Of course not! Or a horst? Ditto! Oh, a geology-lesson at Dieppe college was so many hours wasted! Well, lend me your ears, young Dubosc! I will be brief and to the point. The terrestrial rind—that is, the crust which surrounds the internal fire-ball, of solidified elements and eruptive or sedimentary rocks—consists throughout of layers superposed like the pages of a book. Imagine forces of some kind, acting laterally, to compress those layers. There will be corrugations, sometimes actual fractures, the two sides of which, sliding one against the other, will be either raised or depressed. Faults is the name which we give to the fractures that penetrate the terrestrial shell and separate two masses of rock, one of which slides over the plane of fracture. The fault, therefore, reveals an edge, a lower lip produced by the subsidence of the soil, and an upper lip produced by an elevation. Now it happens that suddenly, after thousands and thousands of years, this upper lip, under the action of irresistible tangential forces, will rise, shoot upwards, and form considerable outthrows, to which we give the name of horsts. This is what has just taken place... . There exists in France, marked on the geological charts, a fault known as the Rouen fault, which is an important dislocation of the Paris basin. Parallel to the corrugations of the soil, which have wrinkled the cretaceous and tertiary deposits in this region from north-east to north-west, it runs from Versailles to seventy-five miles beyond Rouen. At Maromme, we lose it. But I, Simon, have found it again in the quarries above Longueville and also not far from Dieppe. And lastly I have found it ... where do you think? In England, at Eastbourne, between Hastings and Newhaven! Same composition, same disposition. There was no question of a mistake. It ran from France to England! It ran under the Channel. ... Ah, how I have studied it, my fault, Old Sandstone's fault, as I used to call it! How I have sounded it, deciphered its meanings, questioned it, analysed it! And then, suddenly in 1912, some seismic shocks affected the table-lands of the Seine-Inférieure and the Somme and acted in an abnormal manner as I was able to prove—on the tides! Shocks in Normandy! In the Somme! Right out at sea! Do you grasp the strangeness of such a phenomenon and how, on the other hand, it acquired a significant value from the very fact that it took place along a fault? Might we not suppose that there were stresses along this fault, that captive forces were seeking to escape through the earth's crust and attacking the points of least resistance, which happened to lie precisely along the lines of the faults? ... You may call it an improbable theory. Perhaps so; but at any rate it seemed worth verifying. And I did verify it. I made diving-experiments within sight of the French coast. At my fourth descent, in the Ridin de Dieppe, where the depth is only thirty feet, I discovered traces of an eruption in the two blocks of a fault all of whose elements tallied with those of the Anglo-Norman fault ... That was all I wanted to know. There was nothing more to do but wait ... a century or two ... or else a few hours. ... Meanwhile it was patent to me that sooner or later the fragile obstacle opposed to the internal energies would break down and the great upheaval would come to pass. It has come to pass."

Simon listened with growing interest. Old Sandstone illustrated his lecture with diagrams drawn with broad strokes of the pen and smeared with blots which his sleeve or fingers generously spread all over the paper. Drops of sweat also played their part, falling from his forehead, for Old Sandstone was always given to perspiring copiously.

He repeated:

"It has come to pass, with a whole train of precursory or concomitant phenomena: submarine eruptions, whirlpools, boats and ships hurled into the air and drawn under by the most terrible suction; and then seismic tremors, more or less marked, cyclones, waterspouts and the devil's own mischief; and then a cataclysm of an earthquake. And immediately afterwards, indeed at the same moment, the shooting up of one lip of the fault, projecting from one coast to the other, over a width of seventy or eighty miles. And then, on the top of it, you, Simon Dubosc, crossing the Channel at a stride. And this perhaps was not the least remarkable fact, my boy, in the whole story."

Simon was silent for some time. Then he said:

"So far, so good. You have explained the emergence of the narrow belt of earth which I walked along and whose width I measured with my eyes, I might say, incessantly. But how do you explain the emergence of this immense region which now fills the Straits of Dover and part of the Channel?"

"Perhaps the Anglo-Norman fault had ramifications in the affected areas?"

"I repeat, I saw only a narrow belt of land."

"That is to say, you saw and crossed only the highest crests of the upheaved region, crests forming a ridge. But this region was thrown up altogether; and you must have noticed that the waves, instead of subsiding, were rolling over miles of beach."

"That is so. Nevertheless the sea was there and is there no longer."

"It is there no longer because it has receded. Phenomena of this extent produce reactions beyond their immediate field of activity and give rise to other phenomena, which in turn react upon the first. And, if this dislocation of the bottom of the Channel has raised one part, it may very well, in some other submarine part, have provoked subsidences and ruptures by which the sea has escaped through the crust. Observe that a reduction of level of six to nine feet was enough to turn those miles of barely covered beach into permanent dry land."

"A supposition, my dear professor."

"Nothing of the sort!" cried Old Sandstone, striking the table with his fists. "Nothing of the sort! I have positive evidence of this also; and I shall publish all my proofs at a suitable moment, which will not be long delayed."

He drew from his pocket the famous locked wallet, whose grease-stained morocco had caught Simon's eye at Newhaven, and declared:

"The truth will emerge from this, my lad, from this wallet in which my notes have been accumulating, four hundred and fifteen notes which must needs serve for reference. For, now that the phenomena has come to pass and all its mysterious causes have been wiped out by the upheaval, people will never know anything except what I have observed by personal experiments. They will put forward theories, draw inferences, form conclusions. *But they will not see.* Now I . . . have *seen.*"

Simon, who was only half listening, interrupted:

"In the meantime, my dear professor, I am hungry. Will you have some dinner?"

"No, thanks. I must catch the train to Dover and cross to-night. It seems the Calais-Dover boats are running again; and I have no time to lose if I'm to publish an article and take up a definite position." He glanced at his watch. "Phew! It's jolly late! . . . If only I don't lose my train! . . . See you soon, my boy!" . . .

He departed.

The other person sitting in the dark had not stirred during this conversation and, to Simon's great astonishment, did not stir either after Old Sandstone had taken his leave. Simon, at switching on the light, was amazed to find himself face to face with an individual resembling in every respect the man whose body he had seen near the wreck on the previous evening. There was the same brick-red face, the same prominent cheek-bones, the same long hair, the same buff leather clothing. This man, however, was very much younger, with a noble bearing and a handsome face.

"A true Indian chief," thought Simon, "and it seems to me that I have seen him before. . . . Yes, I have certainly seen him somewhere. But where? And when?"

The stranger was silent. Simon asked him:

"What can I do for you, please?"

The other had risen to his feet. He went to the little table on which Simon had emptied his pockets, took up the coin with the head of Napoleon I. which Simon had found the day before and, speaking excellent French, but in a voice whose guttural tone harmonized with his appearance, said:

"You picked up this coin yesterday, on your way here, near a dead body, did you not?"

His guess was so correct and so unexpected that Simon could but confirm it:

"I did . . . near a man who had just been stabbed to death."

"Perhaps you were able to trace the murderer's footprints?"

"Yes."

"They were prints of bathing-shoes or tennis-shoes, with patterned rubber soles?"

"Yes, yes!" said Simon, more and more puzzled. "But how do you know that?"

"Well, sir," continued the man whom Simon silently called the Indian, without replying to the question, "Well, sir, yesterday one of my friends, Badiarinos by name, and his niece Dolores, wishing to explore the new land after the convulsions of the morning, discovered, in the harbor, amid the ruins, a narrow channel which communicated with the sea and was still free at that moment. A man who was getting into a boat offered to take my friend and his niece along with him. After rowing for some time, they saw several large wrecks and landed. Badiarinos left his niece in the boat and went off in one direction, while their companion took another. An hour later, the latter returned alone, carrying an old broken cashbox with gold escaping from it. Seeing blood on one of his sleeves, Dolores became alarmed and tried to get out of the boat. He flung himself upon her and, in spite of her desperate resistance, succeeded in tying her up. He took the oars again and turned back along the new coast-line. On the way, he decided to get rid of her and threw her overboard. She had the good luck to fall on a sandbank which became uncovered a few minutes later and which was soon joined to the mainland. For all that, she would have been dead if you had not released her."

"Yes," murmured Simon, "a Spaniard, isn't she? Very beautiful. ... I saw her again at the casino."

"We spent the whole evening," continued the Indian, in the same impassive tones, "hunting for the murderer, at the meeting in the casino, in the bars of the hotels, in the public-houses, everywhere. This morning we began again ... and I came here, wishing also to bring you the coat which you had lent to my friend's niece."

"It was you, then? ..."

"Now, on entering the corridor upon which your room opens, I heard someone groaning and I saw, a little way ahead of me—the corridor is very dark—I saw a man dragging himself along the floor, wounded, half-dead. A servant and I carried him into one of the rooms which are being used for infirmary purposes; and I could see that he had been stabbed between the shoulders ... as my friend was! Was I on the track of the murderer? It was difficult to make enquiries in this great hotel, crammed with the mixed crowd of people who have come here for shelter. At last I discovered that, a little before nine o'clock, a lady's maid, coming from outside, with a letter in her hand, had asked the porter for M. Simon Dubosc. The porter replied, 'Second floor, room 44.'"

"But I haven't had that letter!" Simon remarked.

"The porter, luckily for you, mistook the number. You're in room 43."

"And what became of it? Who sent it?"

"Here is a piece of the envelope which I picked up," replied the Indian. "You can still make out a seal with Lord Bakefield's arms. So I went to Battle House."

"And you saw ... ?"

"Lord Bakefield, his wife and his daughter had left for London this morning, by motor. But I saw the maid, the one who had been to the hotel with a letter for you from her mistress. As she was going upstairs, she was overtaken by a gentleman who said, 'M. Simon Dubosc is asleep and said I was to let no one in. I'll give him the letter.' The maid therefore handed him the letter and accepted a tip of a louis. Here's the louis. It's one with the head of Napoleon

I. and the date 1807 and is therefore precisely similar to the coin which you picked up near my friend's body."

"And then?" asked Simon, anxiously. "Then this man . . . ?"

"The man, having read the letter, went and knocked at room 44, which is the next room to yours. Your neighbor opened the door and was seized by the throat, while the murderer, with his free arm, drove a dagger into his neck, above the shoulders."

"Do you mean to say that he was stabbed instead of me? . . ."

"Yes, instead of you. But he is not dead. They will pull him through."

Simon was stunned.

"It's dreadful!" he muttered. "Again, that particular way of striking! . . ."

After a short pause, he asked:

"Do you know nothing of the contents of the letter?"

"From some words exchanged by Lord Bakefield and his daughter the maid gathered that they were discussing the wreck of the *Queen Mary*, the steamer on which Miss Bakefield had been shipwrecked the other day and which must be lying high and dry by now. Miss Bakefield appears to have lost a miniature."

"Yes," said Simon, thoughtfully, "yes, I dare say. But it is most distressing that this letter was not placed in my own hands. The maid ought never to have given it up."

"Why should she have been suspicious?"

"What! Of the first person she met?"

"But she knew him."

"She knew this man?"

"Certainly. She had often seen him at Lord Bakefield's; he is a frequent visitor to the house."

"Then she was able to give you his name?"

"She told me his name."

"Well?"

"His name's Rolleston."

Simon gave a start.

"Rolleston!" he exclaimed. "But that's impossible! . . . Rolleston! What madness! . . . What's the fellow like? Give me a description of him."

"The man whom the maid and I saw is very tall, which enables him to bend over his victims and stab them from above between the shoulders. He is thin . . . stoops a little . . . and he's very pale. . . ."

"Stop!" ordered Simon, impressed by this description, which was that of Edward. "Stop! . . . The man is a friend of mine and I'll answer for him as I would for myself. Rolleston a murderer! What nonsense!"

And Simon broke into a nervous laugh, while the Indian, still impassive, resumed:

"Among other matters, the maid told me of a public-house, frequented by rather doubtful people, where Rolleston, a great whiskey-drinker, was a familiar customer. This information was found to be correct. The barman, whom I tipped lavishly, told me that Rolleston had just been there, at about twelve o'clock, that he had enlisted half-a-dozen rascals who were game for anything and that the object of the expedition was the wreck of the *Queen Mary*. I was now fully informed. The whole complicated business was beginning to have a meaning; and I at once made the necessary preparations, though I made a point of coming back here constantly, so that I might be present when you awoke and tell you the news. Moreover, I took care that your friend, Mr. Sandstone, should watch over you; and I locked your pocketbook, which was lying there for anybody to help himself from, in this drawer. I took ten thousand francs out of it to finance our common business."

Simon was past being astonished by the doings of this strange individual. He could have taken all the notes with which the pocketbook was crammed; he had taken only ten. He was at least an honest man.

"Our business?" said Simon. "What do you mean by that?"

"It will not take long to explain, M. Dubosc," replied the Indian, speaking as a man who knows beforehand that he has won his cause. "It's this. Miss Bakefield lost, in the wreck of the *Queen Mary*, a miniature of the greatest value; and her letter was asking you to go and look for it. The letter was intercepted by Rolleston, who was thus informed of the existence of this precious object and at the same time, no doubt, became acquainted with Miss Bakefield's feelings towards you. If we admit that Rolleston, as the maid declares, is in love with Miss Bakefield, this in itself explains his pleasant intention of stabbing you. At any rate, after recruiting half-a-dozen blackguards of the worst kind, he set out for the wreck of the *Queen Mary*. Are you going to leave the road clear for him, M. Dubosc?"

Simon did not at once reply. He was thinking. How could he fail to be struck by the logic of the facts that had come to his notice? Nor could he forget Rolleston's habits, his way of living, his love of whisky and his general extravagance. Nevertheless, he once more asserted;

"Rolleston is incapable of such a thing."

"All right," said the Indian. "But certain men have set out to seize the *Queen Mary*. Are you going to leave the road clear for them? I'm not. I have the death of my friend Badiarinos to avenge. You have Miss Bakefield's letter to bear in mind. We will make a start then. Everything is arranged. Four of my comrades have been notified. I have bought arms, horses and enough provisions to last us. I repeat, everything is ready. What are you going to do?"

Simon threw off his dressing-gown and snatched at his clothes:

"I shall come with you."

"Oh, well," said the Indian smiling, "if you imagine that we can venture on the new land in the middle of the night! What about the water-courses? And the quicksands? And all the rest of it? To say nothing of the devil's own fog! No, no, we shall start to-morrow morning, at four o'clock. In the meantime, eat, M. Dubosc, and sleep."

Simon protested:

"Sleep! Why, I've done nothing else since yesterday!"

"That's not enough. You have undergone the most terrible exertions; and this will be a trying expedition, very trying and very dangerous. You can take Lynx-Eye's word for it."

"Lynx-Eye?"

"Antonio or Lynx-Eye: those are my names," explained the Indian. "Then to-morrow morning, M. Dubosc!"

Simon obeyed like a child. Since they had been living for the past few days in such a topsy-turvy world, could he do better than follow the advice of a man whom he had never seen, who was a Red Indian and who was called Lynx-Eye?

When he had had his meal, he glanced through an evening paper. There was an abundance of news, serious and contradictory. It was stated that Southampton and Le Havre were blocked. It was said that the British fleet was immobilized at Portsmouth. The rivers, choked at their mouths, were overflowing their banks. Everywhere all was disorder and confusion; communications were broken, harbors were filled with sand, ships were lying on their sides, trade was interrupted; everywhere devastation reigned and famine and despair; the local authorities were impotent and the governments distraught.

It was late when Simon at last fell into a troubled sleep.

It seemed to him that after an hour or two some one opened the door of his room; and he remembered that he had not bolted it. Light footsteps crossed the carpet. Then he had the impression that some one bent over him and that this some one was a woman. A cool breath caressed his face and in the darkness he divined a shadow moving quickly away.

He tried to switch on the light, but there was no current.

The shadow left the room. Was it the young woman whom he had released, who had come? But why should she have come?

CHAPTER VIII

ON THE WAR-PATH

At four o'clock in the morning, the streets were almost empty. A few fruit and vegetable-carts were making their way between the demolished houses and the shattered pavements. But from a neighboring avenue there emerged a little cavalcade in which Simon immediately recognized, at the head of the party, astride a monstrous big horse, Old Sandstone, wearing his rusty top-hat, with the skirts of his black frock-coat overflowing either side of a saddle with bulging saddle-bags.

Next came Antonio, *alias* Lynx-Eye, likewise mounted; then a third horseman, perched like the others behind heavy saddle-bags; and lastly three persons on foot, one of whom held the bridle of a fourth horse. The three pedestrians had brick-red faces and long hair and were dressed in the same style as Lynx-Eye, in soft leggings with leather fringes, velveteen breeches, flannel girdles, wide-brimmed felt hats, with gaudy ribbons: in short, a heterogeneous, picturesque band, with many-colored accoutrements, in which the adornments dear to circus cow-boys were displayed side by side with those of one of Fenimore Cooper's Redskins, or one of Gustave Aymard's scouts. They carried rifles slung across their shoulders and revolvers and daggers in their belts.

"What the deuce!" exclaimed Simon. "Why, this is a martial progress! Are we going among savages?"

"We are going into a country," replied Antonio, gravely, "Where there are no inhabitants, no inns, no victuals, but where there are already visitors as dangerous as beasts of prey, which is why we have to carry two days' provisions and two days' supply of oats and compressed fodder for our mounts. This, then, is our escort. These are the brothers Mazzani, the elder and the younger. This is Forsetta. Here is Mr. Sandstone. Here, on horseback, is one of my personal friends. And here, lastly, for you, is Orlando III. a half-breed by Gracious out of Chiquita."

And, at a sign from the Indian, a noble animal was led forward, lean, sinewy and nervous, standing very high on its long legs.

Simon mounted, much amused:

"And you, my dear professor?" he said to Old Sandstone: "Are you one of the party?"

"I lost my train," said the old fellow, "and on returning to the hotel I met Lynx-Eye, who recruited me. I represent science and am entrusted with the geological, geographical, crographical, stratigraphical, palaeontological and other observations. I shall have plenty to do."

"Forward, then!" commanded Simon. And, taking the lead with Antonio, he at once said, "Now tell me about your companions. And you, Lynx-Eye, where do *you* hail from? After all, if there are still a few specimens of Redskins left, they're not out for a good time on the highways of Europe. Confess that you are, all of you, made up and disguised."

"They are no more made up than I am," said Antonio. "We come from the other side. For my part, I am the grandson of one of the last remaining Indian chiefs, Long Carbine who ran away with the little daughter of a Canadian trapper. My mother was a Mexican. You see that, though there's a mixture, our origins are beyond dispute."

"But afterwards, Lynx-Eye? What has happened afterwards? I'm not aware that the British government provides for the descendants of the Sioux or Mohicans?"

"There are other concerns besides the British government," said the Indian.

"What do you mean?"

"I mean there are concerns which are interested in keeping us going."

"Really? What are they?"

"The cinema-firms."

Simon struck his hand against his forehead:

"What an idiot I am! Why didn't I think of that? Then you are. . . ."

"Simply film actors from the Far West, the Prairies and the Mexican frontier."

"That's it! That's it!" cried Simon. "I have seen you on the screen, haven't I? And I've seen . . . hold on. I remember now, I've seen the fair Dolores also, haven't I? But what are you doing in Europe?"

"An English company sent for me and I engaged a few friends over there, who, like myself, are the very mixed descendants of Red Indians, Mexicans and Spaniards. Now, M. Dubosc, one of these friends of mine—the best, for I can't say much for the others, and I advise you, if the occasion should arise, to be very careful with Forsetta and the Mazzani brothers—the best, M. Dubosc, was murdered the day before yesterday by Rolleston. I loved Badiarinos as a son loves his father. I have sworn to avenge him. There you have it."

"Lynx-Eye, grandson of Long Carbine," said Simon, "we will avenge your friend, but Rolleston is not guilty of his murder. . . ."

For a man like Simon, to whom practical navigation, in the air or on the sea, had given a keen sense of direction and who, moreover, kept on consulting his compass, it was child's play to reach a spot whose latitude and longitude he was able to determine more or less exactly. He galloped due south, after making the calculation that, if nothing forced them to turn aside, they would have to cover a distance of about thirty miles.

Almost immediately, the little troop, leaving on their left the line of ridges which Simon had followed a few days before, struck off across a series of rather lower sand-hills, which nevertheless were high enough to overlook immense beds of yellow mud, covered with a network of small, winding streams. This was the slime deposited by the rivers of the coast and carried out to sea by the tides and currents.

"Grand alluvial soil," said Old Sandstone. "The water will form channels for itself. The sandy parts will be absorbed."

"In five years," said Simon, "we shall see herds of cattle grazing on the very bed of the sea; and five years later there will be railway-lines across it and palatial hotels standing in the middle."

"Perhaps; but, for the moment the situation is not promising," observed the old professor. "Look here, look at this newspaper, published yesterday evening. In both France and England the disorder is complete. Social and economic life has been suddenly paralyzed. No more public services. Letters and telegrams may or may not be delivered. Nothing definite is known; and people are saying the most extraordinary things. The cases of insanity and suicide, it seems, are numberless. And the crimes! Isolated crimes, crimes committed by gangs of criminals, riots, shops and churches pillaged wholesale. It's an absolute chaos; we are back in the dark ages."

The stratum of mud, formerly swept by the ground-wash, was not very thick; and they were able, time after time, to venture upon it without the least danger. For that matter, it was already indented with footprints, which also marked the still moist sand of the hills. They passed the hulk of a steamboat round which some people had established a sort of camp. Some were poking about the hull. Others were entering by the battered funnel, or demolishing the woodwork with hammers, or breaking open cases of more or less intact provisions. Women of the people, women in rags and tatters, wearing the look of hunted animals, sat on pieces of timber, waiting. Children ran about, playing; and already, marking a first attempt at communal life, a pedlar was moving through the crowd with a keg of beer on his back, while two girls, installed behind a tottering bar, were selling tea and whisky.

Farther on, they saw a second camp and, in all directions, men prowling about, solitary individuals, who, like themselves, were reconnoitring.

"Capital!" cried Simon. "The prairie lies stretched before us, with all its mysteries and all its lurking dangers. Here we are on the war-path; and the man who leads us is a Red Indian chief."

After they had trotted for two hours at a brisk pace, the prairie was represented by undulating plains, in which sand and mud alternated in equal proportions and in which hesitating streams of no great depth were seeking a favorable bed. Over it hung a low, thick, stationary fog, apparently as solid as a ceiling.

"What a miracle, my dear Old Sandstone!" cried Simon, while they were following a long ribbon of fine gravel which stretched before them, like a sunken path winding through the greensward of a park. "What a miracle, an adventure of this sort! A horrible adventure, certainly; a disaster causing superhuman suffering, death and mourning; but extraordinary adventure, the finest that a man of my age could dream of. It's all so prodigious!"

"Prodigious, indeed!" said Old Sandstone, who, faithful to his mission, was pursuing his scientific investigations. "Prodigious! Thus, the presence of this gravel in this place constitutes one of the unprecedented events of which you are speaking. And then look at that bank of great golden fish lying over there, with their upturned bellies. . . ."

"Yes, yes, professor," replied Simon. "It's impossible that such an upheaval should not usher in a new age! If I look at the future as people sometimes look at a landscape, with my eyes half-closed, I can see . . . heavens, what don't I see! . . . What don't I imagine! . . . What a tragedy of folly, passion, hatred, love, violence, and noble efforts! We are entering upon one of those periods in which men are full to overflowing of energy, in which the will goes to the head like a generous wine!"

The young man's enthusiasm ended by annoying Old Sandstone, who moved away from his expansive companion, grumbling:

"Simon, the memory of Fenimore Cooper is making you lose your head. You're getting too talkative, my son."

Simon was not losing his head, but he was possessed by a burning fever and, after the hours which he had experienced two days before, was quivering with impatience to return, so to speak, to the world of abnormal actions.

In point of fact, Isabel's image was before him in all his thoughts and in all his dreams. He paid hardly any attention to the precise aim of his expedition or to the campaign which they were undertaking to recover a certain object. The precious miniature was hidden in the rug where he was sure to find it. Rolleston? His gang of ruffians? Men stabbed in the back? A pack of inventions and nightmares! The only reality was Isabel. The only aim before him was to distinguish himself as a knight fighting for the love of his lady.

Meanwhile there were no longer any camps around wrecks, nor parties of people searching for valuables, but only individual prowlers and very few of these, as though most of the people were afraid to go too far from the coast. The surface was becoming more broken, consisting, no doubt, as Old Sandstone explained, of former sand banks which the seismic disturbances had shaken down and mixed with the underlying sedimentary strata. They had to go out of their way to avoid not shattered rocks indeed, nor compact cliffs, but raised tracts of ground that had not yet assumed those definite forms in which we perceive the action of time, of time which separates, classifies and discriminates, which organizes chaos and gives it a durable aspect.

They crossed a sheet of perfectly clear water, contained within a circle of low hills. The bottom was carpeted with little white pebbles. Then they descended, between two very high banks of mud, a narrow gully through which the water trickled in slender cascades. As they emerged from this gully, the Indian's horse shied. A man was kneeling on the ground, groaning and writhing in pain, his face covered with blood. Another man lay near him, his white face turned to the sky.

Antonio and Simon at once sprang from their horses. When the wounded man raised his head, Simon cried:

"Why, I know him . . . it's Williams, Lord Bakefield's secretary. And I know the other too: it's Charles, the valet. They have been attacked. What is it, Williams? You know me, Simon Dubosc."

The man could hardly speak. He spluttered:

"Bakefield . . . Lord Bakefield. . . ."

"Come, Williams, tell me what happened?"

"Yesterday . . . yesterday. . . ." replied the secretary.

"Yes, yesterday you were attacked. By whom?"

"Rolleston. . . ."

Simon started:

"Rolleston! Did he kill Charles?"

"Yes. . . . I. . . . I was wounded. . . . I have been calling out all night. And, just now, another man. . . ."

Antonio put a question:

"You were attacked again, were you not, by some thief who wanted to rob you. . . . And, when he heard us coming, he too stabbed you and took to his heels? Then he is not far away?"

"There . . . there," stammered Williams, trying to stretch out his arm.

The Indian pointed to footsteps which led to the left, up the slope of the hills:

"There's the trail," he said.

"I'll follow it up," said Simon, leaping into the saddle.

The Indian protested:

"What's the use?"

"Use? The scoundrel must be punished!"

Simon went off at a gallop, followed by one of the Indian's companions, the one who rode the fourth horse and whose name he did not know. Almost immediately, at five hundred yards ahead, on the ridge of the hills, a man rose from the cover of some blocks of stone and made away at the top of his speed.

Two minutes later, Simon reached these blocks and exclaimed:

"I see him! He's going around the lake which we crossed. Let's make straight for him."

He descended the farther slope and forced his horse into the water, which, at this point, covered a layer of mud so deep that the two riders had some difficulty in getting clear of it. When they reached the opposite shore, the fugitive, seeing that there were only two of them, turned round, threw up his rifle and covered them:

"Halt," he commanded, "or I fire!"

Simon was going too fast and could not pull up.

At the moment when the shot rang, he was at most twenty yards from the murderer. But another rider had leapt between them and was holding his horse, reared on its hind legs, like a rampart in front of Simon. The animal was hit in the belly and fell.

"Thanks, old chap, you've saved my life!" cried Simon, abandoning the pursuit and dismounting to succour the other, who was in an awkward position, jammed under his horse and in danger of being kicked by the dying brute.

Nevertheless, when Simon endeavoured to extricate him, the fallen rider did nothing to assist his efforts; and, after releasing him with some difficulty, he perceived that the man had fainted.

"That's odd!" thought Simon. "Those fellows don't usually faint over a fall from a horse!"

He knelt down beside the other and, seeing that his breathing was embarrassed, undid the first few buttons of his shirt and uncovered the upper part of his chest. He was stupefied and for the first time looked at his companion, who hitherto, in the shadow of his broad-brimmed hat, had seemed to him like the other Indians of the escort. The hat had fallen off. Quickly, Simon lifted an orange silk kerchief bound round the head and neck of the supposed Red Indian, whose hair escaped from it in thick black curls.

"The girl!" he muttered. "Dolores!"

Once more he had before his eyes the vision of radiant beauty to which his mind had recurred several times during the past two days, though no emotion mingled with his admiration. He was so far from any thought of concealing this admiration that the young woman, on recovering consciousness, surprised it in his gaze. She smiled:

"I'm all right now!" she said. "I was only stunned."

"You're not in pain?"

"No. I am used to accidents. I've often had to fall from my horse for the films. . . . This one's dead, isn't he? Poor creature!"

"You've saved my life," said Simon.

"We're quits," she replied.

Her expression was grave and harmonized with her slightly austere features. Her's was one of those beautiful faces which are peculiarly disconcerting by reason of the contrasts which they present, being at once passionate and chaste, noble and sensuous, pensive and enticing.

Simon asked her, point blank:

"Was it you who came to my room yesterday, first in broad daylight and afterwards at night?"

She blushed, but admitted:

"Yes, it was I."

And, at a movement of Simon's, she added:

"I felt uneasy. People were being killed, in town and in the hotel. I had to watch over you, who had saved my life."

"I thank you," he said once more.

"Don't thank me. I have been doing things in spite of myself . . . these last two days. You seem to me so different from other men! . . . But I ought not to speak to you like this. Don't be vexed with me!"

Simon held out his hand to her, when suddenly she assumed a listening attitude and then, after a moment's attention, straightened her clothes, hid her hair beneath her kerchief and put on her hat.

"It's Antonio," she said, in a different tone. "He must have heard the firing. Don't let him know that you recognized me, will you?"

"Why?" asked Simon, in surprise.

She replied, in some embarrassment:

"It's better. . . . Antonio is very masterful. He forbade me to come. It was only when he was naming the three Indians of the escort that he recognized me; I had taken the fourth Indian's horse. . . . So, you see. . . ."

She did not complete her sentence. A horseman had made his appearance on the ridge. When he came up to them, Dolores had unfastened her saddle-bags and was strapping them to the saddle of Simon's horse. Antonio asked no questions. There was no exchange of explanations. With a glance he reconstructed the scene, examined the dead animal and, addressing the young woman by her name, perhaps to show that he was not taken in, said:

"Have my horse, Dolores."

Was it the mere familiarity of a comrade, or that of a man who wishes, in the presence of another man, to assert his rights or his pretentions to a woman? His tone was not imperious, but Simon surprised the glance that flashed anger on the one side and defiance on the other. However, he paid little attention, being much less anxious to discover the private motives which actuated Dolores and Antonio than to elucidate the problem arising from his meeting with Lord Bakefield's secretary.

"Did Williams say anything?" he asked Antonio, who was beside him.

"No, he died without speaking."

"Oh! He's dead! . . . And you discovered nothing?"

"Nothing."

"Then what do you think? Were Williams and Charles sent to the *Queen Mary* by Lord Bakefield and his daughter and were they to find me and help me in my search? Or did they go on their own account?"

They soon joined the three pedestrians of the escort, to whom Old Sandstone, with a cluster of shells in his hand, was giving a geological lesson. The three pedestrians were asleep.

"I'm going ahead," said Antonio to Simon. "Our horses need a rest. In an hour's time, set out along the track of the white pebbles which I shall drop as I go. You can ride at a trot. My three comrades are good runners."

He had already gone some paces, when he returned and, drawing Simon aside, looked him straight in the eyes and said:

"Be on your guard with Dolores, M. Dubosc. She is one of these women of whom it is wise to beware. I have seen many a man lose his head over her."

Simon smiled and could not refrain from saying:

"Perhaps Lynx-Eye is one of them?"

The Indian repeated:

"Be on your guard, M. Dubosc!"

And with these words he went his way. They seemed to sum up all that he thought of Dolores.

Simon ate, stretched himself out on the ground and smoked some cigarettes. Sitting on the sand, Dolores unpicked a few seams of the wide trousers which she was wearing and arranged them in such a fashion that they might have been taken for a skirt.

An hour later, as Simon was making ready to start, his attention was attracted by a sound of voices. At some little distance, Dolores and one of the three Indians were standing face to face and disputing in a language which Simon did not understand, while the brothers Mazzani were watching them and grinning.

Dolores' arms were folded across her breast; she stood motionless and scornful. The man, on the contrary, was gesticulating, with a snarling face and glittering eyes. Suddenly he took both Dolores' arms and, drawing her close to him, sought her lips.

Simon leapt to his feet. But there was no need of intervention; the Indian had at once recoiled, pricked at the throat by a dagger which Dolores held before her, the handle pressed against her bosom, the point threatening her adversary.

The incident was not followed by any sort of explanation. The Indian made off, grumbling. Old Sandstone, who had seen nothing, tackled Simon on the subject of his geological fault; and Simon merely said to himself, as Dolores tightened her saddle-girth:

"What the deuce are all these people up to?"

He did not waste time in seeking for an answer to the question.

The little band did not overtake Antonio until three hours later, when he was stooping over the ground, examining some footprints.

"There you are," he said to Simon, straightening his back. "I have made out thirteen distinct tracks, left by people who certainly were not travelling together. In addition to these thirteen highwaymen—for a man has to be a pretty tough lot to risk the journey—there are two parties ahead of us: first, a party of four horsemen and then, walking behind them—how many hours later I couldn't say—a party of seven on foot, forming Rolleston's gang. Look, here's the print of the patterned rubber soles."

"Yes, yes," said Simon, recognizing the footprint which he had seen two days before. "And what do you conclude?"

"I conclude that Rolleston, as we knew, is in it and that all these gentry, separate prowlers and parties, are making for the *Queen Mary*, the last large Channel boat sunk and the nearest to this part of the coast. Think, what a scoop for marauders!"

"Let's push on!" cried the young man, who was now uneasy at the thought that he might fail in the mission which Isabel had allotted to him.

One by one, five other tracks coming from the north—from Eastbourne, the Indian thought—joined the first. In the end they made such an intricate tangle that Antonio had to give up counting them. However, the footprints of the rubber soles and those of the four horses continued to appear in places.

They marched on for some time. The landscape showed little variety, revealing sandy plains and hills, stretches of mud, rivers and pools, of water left by the sea and filled with fish which had taken refuge there. It was all monotonous, without beauty or majesty, but strange, as anything that has never been seen before or anything that is shapeless must needs be strange.

"We are getting near," said Simon.

"Yes," said the Indian, "the tracks are coming in from all directions; and here even are marauders returning northwards, laden with their swag."

It was now four in the afternoon. Not a rift was visible in the ceiling of motionless clouds. Rain fell in great, heavy drops. For the first time they heard the overhead roar of an aeroplane flying above the insuperable obstacle. . . . They followed a depression in the ground, succeeded by hills. And suddenly a bulky object rose before them. It was the *Queen Mary*. She was bent in two, almost like a broken toy. And nothing was more lamentable, nothing gave a more dismal impression of ruin and destruction than those two lifeless halves of a once so powerful thing.

There was no one near the wreck.

Simon experienced an extreme emotion on standing before what was left of the big boat which he had seen wrecked so terribly. He could not approach it without that sort of pious horror which one would feel on entering a mighty tomb haunted by the shades of those whom we once knew. He thought of the three clergymen and the French family and the captain; and he shuddered at remembering the moment when, with all the strength of his will and all the imperious power of his love, he had dragged Isabel towards the abyss.

A halt was called. Simon left his horse with the Indians and went forward, accompanied by Antonio. He ran down the steep slope which the stern of the vessel had hollowed in the sand, gripped with both hands a rope which hung beside the rudder and in a few seconds, with the assistance of his feet and knees, reached the stern rail.

Although the deck had listed violently to starboard and a sticky mud was oozing through the planking, he ran to the spot where Isabel and he had sat. The bench had been torn away, but the iron supports were still standing and the rug which she had slung to one of them was there, shrunk, heavy with the water dripping from it and packed, as before the shipwreck, in its straps, which were untouched.

Simon thrust his hand between the wet folds of the rug, as he had seen Isabel do. Not feeling anything, he tried to unfasten the straps, but the leather had swollen and the ends were jammed in the buckles. Then he took his knife, cut the straps and unrolled the rug. The miniature in its pearl setting was gone.

In its place, fixed with a safety-pin, was a sheet of paper.

He unfolded it. On it were these hastily-written words, which Isabel evidently intended for him:

"I was hoping to see you. Haven't you received my letter? We have spent the night here—in an absolute hell on earth! and we are just leaving. I am uneasy. I feel that some one is prowling around us. Why are not you here?"

"Oh!" Simon stammered, "it's incredible!"

He showed the note to Antonio, who had joined him, and at once added:

"Miss Bakefield! . . . She spent the night here . . . with her father . . . and they have gone! But where? How are we to save them from so many lurking dangers?"

The Indian read the letter and said, slowly:

"They have not gone back north. I should have seen their tracks."

"Then. . . . ?"

"Then. . . . I don't know."

"But this is awful! See, Antonio, think of all that is threatening them . . . of Rolleston pursuing them! Think of this wild country, swarming with highwaymen and foot-pads! . . . It's horrible, horrible!"

PART THE SECOND

CHAPTER I

INSIDE THE WRECK

The expedition so gaily launched, in which Simon saw merely a picturesque adventure, such as one reads of in novels, had suddenly become the most formidable tragedy. It was no longer a matter of cinema Indians and circus cow-boys, nor of droll discoveries in fabled lands, but of real dangers, of ruthless brigands operating in regions where no organized force could thwart their enterprises. What could Isabel and her father do, beset by criminals of the worst type?

"Good God!" exclaimed Simon. "How could Lord Bakefield be so rash as to risk this journey? Look here, Antonio, the lady's-maid told you that Lord Bakefield had gone to London by train, with his wife and daughter...."

"A misunderstanding," declared the Indian. "He must have seen the duchess to the station and arranged the expedition with Miss Bakefield."

"Then they're alone, those two?"

"No, they have two men-servants with them. It's the four riders whose tracks we picked up."

"What imprudence!"

"Imprudence, yes. Miss Bakefield told you of it in the intercepted letter, counting on you to take the necessary measures to protect her. Moreover, Lord Bakefield had given orders to his secretary, Williams, and his valet, Charles, to join them. That is why those two poor fellows were put out of action on the road by Rolleston and his six accomplices."

"Those are the men I'm afraid of," said Simon, hoarsely. "Have Lord Bakefield and his daughter escaped them? Did the departure of which Miss Bakefield speaks take place before their arrival? How can we find out? Where are we to look for them?"

"Here," said Antonio.

"On this deserted wreck?"

"There's a whole crowd inside the wreck," the Indian affirmed. "Here, we'll begin by questioning the boy who is watching us over there."

Leaning against the stump of a broken mast, stood a lean, pasty-faced gutter-snipe, with his hands in his pockets, smoking a huge cigar. Simon went up to him, muttering:

"Very like one of Lord Bakefield's favorite Havanas.... Where did you sneak that cigar?" he asked.

"I ain't sneaked nuffin, sure as my name's Jim. It was giv' me."

"Who gave it you?"

"My old man."

"Where is he, your old man?"

"Listen...."

They listened. A noise echoed beneath their feet in the bowels of the wreck. It sounded like the regular blows of a hammer.

"That's my old man, smashin' 'er up," said the urchin, grinning.

"Tell me," said Simon, "have you seen an elderly gentleman and a young lady who came here on horseback?"

"Dunno," said the boy, carelessly. "Ask my old man."

Simon drew Antonio to where a companion-ladder led from the deck to the first-class cabins, as a still legible inscription informed them. They were going down the ladder when Simon, leading the way, struck his foot against something and nearly fell. By the light of a pocket-torch he saw the dead body of a woman. Though the face, which was swollen and bloated and half eaten away, was unrecognizable, certain signs, such as the color and material of clothes, enabled Simon to identify the French lady whom he had seen with her husband and children. On stooping, he saw that the left hand had been severed at the wrist and that two fingers were lacking on the right hand.

"Poor woman!" he faltered. "Unable to remove her rings and bracelets, the blackguards mutilated her!" And he added. "To think that Isabel was here, that night, in this hell!"

The corridor which they entered as they followed the sound of hammering led them astern. At a sudden turning a man appeared, holding in his hand a lump of iron with which he was striking furiously at the partition-wall of a cabin. Through the ground-glass panes in the ceiling filtered a pale white light which fell full upon the most loathsome face imaginable, a scoundrelly, pallid, cruel face, with a pair of bloodshot eyes and an absolutely bald skull dripping with sweat.

"Keep your distance, mates! Everybody do the best he can in his own! There's plenty of stuff to go round!"

"The old man ain't much of a talker," said the urchin's shrill voice.

The boy had accompanied them and stood, with a bantering air, puffing great whiffs of smoke. The Indian handed him a fifty-franc note:

"Jim, you have something to tell us. Out with it."

"That's all right," said the boy. "I'm beginnin' to twig this business. Come along 'ere!"

Guided by the boy, Antonio and Simon passed along other corridors where they found the same fury of destruction. Everywhere fierce-looking ruffians were forcing locks, tearing, splitting, smashing, looting. Everywhere they were seen creeping into dark corners, crawling on their hands and knees, sniffing out booty and seeking, in default of gold or silver, bits of leather or scrap-metal that might prove marketable.

They were beasts of prey, carrion brutes, like those which prowl about a battlefield. Mutilated and stripped corpses bore witness to their ferocity. There were no rings left upon the bodies, no bracelets, watches, or pocket-books; no pins in the men's ties; no brooches at the women's throats.

From time to time, here and there, in this workyard of death and hideous theft, the sound of a quarrel arose; two bodies rolling on the ground; shouts, yells of pain, ending in the death-rattle. Two plunderers came to grips; and in a moment one of them was a murderer.

Jim halted in front of a roomy cabin, the lower part of whose sloping floor was under water; but on the upper part were several cane-deck chairs which were almost dry.

"That's where they spent the night," he said.

"Who?" asked Simon.

"The three what come on horseback. I was the first on the wreck with my old man. I saw 'em come."

"But there were four of them."

"There was one what lay down outside to guard the horses. The other three went to get something out of the rug where you didn't find nuffin; and they 'ad their grub and slept in 'ere. This mornin', after they left, my old man come to go through the cabin and found the old gent's cigar-case here."

"So they went away again?"

The boy was silent.

"Answer my question, can't you, boy? They left on horseback, didn't they, before the others got here? And they're out of danger?"

The boy held out his hand:

"Two notes," he demanded.

Simon was on the point of flying at him. But he restrained himself, gave the boy the notes and pulled out his revolver:

"Now then!"

The boy shrugged his shoulders:

"It's the notes is making me talk, not that thing! . . . Well, it's like this: when the old gent wanted to start this mornin', he couldn't find the old chap what was guarding the four horses near the stern of the vessel, what you got up by."

"But the horses?"

"Gone!"

"You mean, stolen?"

"'Arf a mo! The old gent, his daughter and the other gent went off to look for him, following the track of the 'osses alongside the wreck. That took them to the other part of the *Queen Mary*, just to the place where the starboard lifeboat was stove in. And then—I was on deck, like I was just now, and I see the whole business as if it was the movies—there was five or six devils got up from behind the lifeboat and rushed at 'em; and a great tall bloke a-leadin' of 'em with a revolver in each fist. I wouldn't say everythink passed off quiet, not on neither side. The old gent, 'e defended himself. There was some shootin'; and I see two of 'em fall in the scrimmage."

"And then? And then?" Simon rapped out, breathlessly.

"I don't know nuffin about then. A change of pickshers, like at the movies. The old man wanted me for somefink; he took me by the scruff o' the neck and I lost the end o' the film like."

It was now Simon's turn to seize the young hooligan by the scruff of the neck. He dragged him up the companion-ladder and, having reached a part of the deck where the whole wreck was visible, he said:

"It was over there, the lifeboat?"

"Yuss, over there."

Simon rushed to the stern of the vessel, slid down the rope and, followed by the Indian and the boy, ran alongside the steamer to the lifeboat which had been torn from the *Queen Mary's* deck and cast on the sands some twenty yards from the wreck. It was here that the attack had taken place. Traces of it remained. The body of one of those whom the boy had described as "devils" was half-hidden in a hollow.

But a cry of pain rose from behind the boat. Simon and the Indian ran round it and saw a man cowering there, with his forehead bound up in a bloodstained handkerchief.

"Rolleston!" cried Simon, stopping short in bewilderment. "Edward Rolleston!"

Rolleston! The man whom all accused! The man who had planned the whole affair and recruited the Hastings blackguards in order to make a dash for the wreck and steal the miniature! Rolleston, the murderer of Dolores' uncle, the murderer of William and Charles! Rolleston, Isabel's persecutor!

Nevertheless Simon hesitated, profoundly troubled by the sight of his friend. Fearing an outburst of anger on the Indian's part, he seized him by the arm:

"Wait a moment, Antonio! . . . First, are you really certain?"

For some seconds, neither stirred. Simon was thinking that Rolleston's presence on the battle-field was the most convincing proof of his guilt. But Antonio declared:

"This is not the man I met in the corridor of the hotel."

"Ah!" cried Simon. "I was sure of it! In spite of all appearances, I could not admit. . . ."

And he rushed up to his friend, saying:

"Wounded, Ted? It's not serious, is it, old man?"

The Englishman murmured:

"Is that you, Simon? I didn't recognize you. My eyes are all misty."

"You're not in pain?"

"I should think I was in pain! The bullet must have struck against the skull and then glanced off; and here I've been since this morning, half dead. But I shall get over it."

Simon questioned him anxiously:

"Isabel? What has become of her?"

"I don't know. . . . I don't know," the Englishman said, with an effort. "No . . . no . . . I don't know. . . ."

"But where do you come from? How do you come to be here?"

"I was with Lord Bakefield and Isabel."

"Ah!" said Simon. "Then you were of their party?"

"Yes. We spent the night on the *Queen Mary* . . . and this morning we were set upon here, by the gang. We were retreating, when I dropped. Lord Bakefield and Isabel fell back on the *Queen Mary*, where it would have been easier for them to defend themselves. Rolleston and his men were not firing at them, however."

"Rolleston?" echoed Simon.

"A cousin of mine . . . Wilfred Rolleston, a damned brute, capable of anything . . . a scoundrel . . . a crook . . . oh, a madman! A real madman . . . a dipsomaniac. . . ."

"And he's like you in appearance isn't he?" asked Simon, understanding the mistake that had been made.

"I suppose so."

"And it was to steal the miniature and the pearls that he attacked you?"

"That . . . and something else that he's even more keen on."

"What?"

"He's in love with Isabel. He asked her to marry him at a time when he hadn't fallen so low. Then Bakefield kicked him out."

"Oh, it would be too awful," stammered Simon, "if that man had succeeded in kidnapping Isabel!"

He stood up. Rolleston, exhausted, said:

"Save her, Simon."

"But you, Ted? We can't leave you. . . ."

"She comes first. He has sworn to have his revenge; he has sworn that Isabel shall be his wife."

"But what are we to do? Where are we to look for her?" cried Simon, in despair.

At that moment Jim came up, all out of breath. He was followed by a man whom Simon at once recognized as a groom in Lord Bakefield's service.

"The bloke!" cried Jim. "The one what looked after the horses. . . . . I found him among the rocks . . . d'you see? Over there? They'd tied him up and the horses were tied up in a sort of cave like. . . ."

Simon lost no time:

"Miss Bakefield?"

"Carried off," replied the man. "Carried off . . . and his lordship as well."

"Ah!" cried Simon, overwhelmed.

The man continued:

"Rolleston is their leader, Wilfred Rolleston. He came up to me this morning at sunrise, as I was seeing to the horses, and asked me if Lord Bakefield was still there. Then, without waiting for an answer, he knocked me flat, with the help of his men, and had me carried here, where they laid an ambush for his lordship. They didn't mind what they said before me; and I learnt that Mr. Williams, the secretary, and Charles, my fellow-servant, who were to have joined us and increased the escort, had been attacked by them and, most likely, killed. I learnt too that Rolleston's idea was to keep Miss Bakefield as a hostage and to send his lordship to his Paris banker's to get the ransom. Later on, they left me alone. Then I heard two shots and, a little after, they returned with his lordship and Miss Bakefield. Both of them had their hands and feet tied."

"At what time did all this happen?" asked Simon, quivering with impatience.

"Nine o'clock, sir, or thereabouts."

"Then they have a day's start of us?"

"Oh, no! There were provisions in the saddle-bags. They sat eating and drinking and then went to sleep. It was at least two o'clock in the afternoon when they strapped his lordship and Miss Bakefield to a couple of horses and started."

"In what direction?"

"That way," said the man-servant, pointing.

"Antonio," cried Simon, "we must catch them before night! The ruffian's escort is on foot. Three hours' gallop will be enough. . . ."

"Our horses are badly done up," objected the Indian.

"They've got to get there, if it kills them."

Simon Dubosc gave the servant his instructions:

"Get Mr. Rolleston under shelter in the wreck, look after him and don't leave him for a second. Jim, can I count on you?"

"Yes."

"And on your father?"

"All depends."

"Fifty pounds for him if the wounded man is in Brighton, safe and sound, in two days' time."

"Make it a hundred," said Jim. "Not a penny less."

"Very well, a hundred."

At six o'clock in the evening, Simon and Antonio returned to the Indians' camp. They quickly bridled and saddled their horses, while Old Sandstone, who was strolling around, ran up to them shouting:

"My fault, Simon! I swear we are over my fault, the fault in the Paris basin, which I traced to Maromme and near the Ridin de Dieppe . . . the one whose fracture caused the whole upheaval. Get on your horse, so that I may give you my proofs. There's a regular Eocene and Pliocene mixture over there which is really typical. . . . Heavens, man, listen to me, can't you?"

Simon stepped up to him and, with drawn features, shouted:

"This is no time to listen to your nonsense!"

"What do you mean?" stammered the old fellow, utterly bewildered.

"Mean? Why, shut up!"

And the young man leapt into the saddle:

"Are you coming, Antonio?"

"Yes. My mates will follow our trail. I shall leave a mark from spot to spot; and I hope we shall all be united again to-morrow."

As they were starting, Dolores, on horseback, brought up her mount alongside theirs.

"No!" said Antonio. "You come on with the others. The professor can't walk all the time."

She made no reply.

"I insist on your keeping with the others," repeated the half-breed, more severely.

But she set her horse at a trot and caught up with Simon.

For more than an hour they followed a direction which Simon took to be south by south-east, that is to say, the direction of France. The half-breed thought the same:

"The main thing," he said, "is to get near the coast, as our beasts have only enough food to last them till to-morrow evening. The water question also might become troublesome."

"I don't care what happens to-morrow," Simon rejoined.

They made much slower progress than they had hoped to do. Their mounts were poor, spiritless stuff. Moreover, they had to stop at intervals to decipher the tracks which crossed one another in the wet sand or to pick them up on rocky ground. Simon became incensed at each of these halts.

All around them the scene was like that which they had observed early in the afternoon; the land rose and fell in scarcely perceptible undulations; it was a dismal, monotonous world, with its graveyards of ships and skeleton steamers. Prowling figures crossed it in all directions. Antonio shouted questions to them as he passed. One of them said that he had met two horsemen and four pedestrians leading a couple of horses on which were bound a man and a woman whose fair hair swept the ground.

"How long ago was this?" asked Simon, in a hoarse voice.

"Forty minutes, or fifty at the most."

He dug his heels into his horse's flanks and set off at a gallop, stooping over the animal's neck in order not to lose the scoundrel's track. Antonio found it difficult to follow him, while Dolores erect in her saddle, with a serious face and eyes fixed on the distant horizon, kept up with him without an effort.

Meanwhile the light was failing, and the riders felt as though the darkness were about to swoop down on them from the heavy clouds in which it was gathering.

"We shall get there . . . we must," repeated Simon. "I feel certain we shall see them in ten minutes. . . ."

He told Dolores in a few words what he had heard of Isabel's abduction. The thought that she was in pain caused unendurable torture. His overwrought mind pictured her a captive among savages torturing her for their amusement, while her blood-bedabbled head was gashed by the stones along the track. He followed in imagination all the stages of her last agony; and he had such a keen impression of speed contending with death, he searched the horizon with so eager a gaze, that he scarcely heeded a strident call from the half-breed, a hundred yards in the rear.

Dolores turned and calmly observed:

"Antonio's horse has fallen."

"Antonio can follow us," said Simon.

For a few moments, they had been riding through a rather more uneven tract of land, covered with a sort of downs with precipitous sides, like cliffs. A fairly steep incline led to a long valley, filled with water, on the brink of which the bandits' trail was plainly visible. They entered the water, making for a place on the opposite edge which seemed to them, at a distance, to be trampled in the same way.

The water, which barely reached the horses' hocks, flowed in a gentle current from left to right. But, when they had covered a third of the distance, Dolores struck Simon's horse with her long reins:

"Hurry!" she commanded. "Look . . . on the left. . . ."

On the left the whole width of the valley was blocked by a lofty wave which was gathering at either end into a long, foaming breaker. It was merely a natural phenomenon; as a result of the great upheaval, the waters were seeking their level and invading the lower tracts. Moreover, the flow was so gradual that there was no reason to fear its effects. The horses, however, seemed to be gradually sinking. Dragged by the current, they were forced to sheer off to the right; and at the same time the opposite bank was moving away from them, changing its aspect, shifting back as the new stream rose. And, when they had reached it, they were still obliged, in order to escape the water, which pursued them incessantly, to quicken their pace and trot along the narrow lane enclosed between two little cliffs of dried mud, in which thousands upon thousands of shells were encrusted like the cubes of a mosaic.

Only after half an hour's riding were they able to clamber to a table-land where they were out of reach. It was as well, for their horses refused to go any farther.

The darkness was increasing. How were they to recover the tracks of Isabel and her kidnappers? And how could their own tracks, buried beneath this enormous sheet of water, be recovered by Antonio and his men?

"We are separated from the others," said Simon, "and I don't see how our party can be got together again."

"Not before to-morrow, at all events," said Dolores.

"Not before. . . ."

And so these two were alone in the night, in the depths of this mysterious land.

Simon strode to and fro on the plateau, like a man who does not know on what course to decide and who knows, moreover, that there is no course on which he can decide. But Dolores unsaddled the horses, unbuckled the saddle-bags and said:

"Our food will hold out, but we have nothing to drink. The spare water-bottles were strapped to Antonio's saddle."

And she added, after spreading out the two horse-rugs:

"We will sleep here, Simon."

CHAPTER II

ALONG THE CABLE

He fell asleep beside her, after a long spell of waking during which his uneasiness was gradually assuaged by the soft and regular rhythm which marked the young girl's breathing.

When he woke, fairly late in the morning, Dolores was stooping and bathing her beautiful arms and her face in the stream that flowed down the hillside. She moved slowly; and all her attitude, as she dried her arms and put back her hair, knotting it low on her neck, were full of a grave harmony.

As Simon stood up, she filled a glass and brought it to him:

"Drink that," she said. "Contrary to what I thought, it's fresh water. I heard our horses drinking it in the night."

"That's easily explained," said Simon. "During the first few days, the rivers of the old coasts filtered in more or less anywhere, until forced, by their increasing flow, to wear themselves a new course. Judging by the direction which this one seems to follow and by its size, it should be a French river, doubtless the Somme, which will join the sea henceforth between Le Havre and Southampton. Unless...."

He was not certain of his argument. In reality, under the implacable veil of the clouds, which were still motionless and hanging very low, and without his compass, which he had heedlessly handed to Antonio, he did not know how to take his bearings. He had followed in Isabel's track last evening; and he hesitated to venture in either direction now that this track was lost and that there was no clue to justify his seeking her in one direction rather than in another.

A discovery of Dolores put an end to his hesitation. In exploring the immediate surroundings, the girl had noticed a submarine cable which crossed the river.

"Capital!" he said. "The cable evidently comes from England, like ourselves. If we follow it, we shall be going towards France.

We shall be sure of going the same way as our enemies and we shall very likely pick up some information on the road."

"France is a long way off," Dolores remarked, "and our horses perhaps won't last for more than another half day."

"That's their lookout," cried Simon. "We shall finish the journey on foot. The great thing is to reach the French coast. Let us make a start."

At two hundred yards' distance, in a depression of the soil, the cable rose from the river and ran straight to a sand-bank, after which it appeared once more, like one of those roads which show in sections on uneven plains.

"It will lead you to Dieppe," said a wandering Frenchman, whom Simon had stopped. "I've just come from there. You've only to follow it."

They followed it in silence. A mute companion, speaking none save indispensable words, Dolores seemed to be always self-absorbed, or to heed only the horses and the details of the expedition. As for Simon, he gave no thought to her. It was a curious fact that he had not yet felt, even casually, that there was something strange and disturbing in the adventure that brought him, a young man, and her, a young woman, together. She remained the unknown; yet this mystery had no particular attraction for him, nor did Antonio's enigmatic words recur to his memory. Though he was perfectly well aware that she was very beautiful, though it gave him pleasure to look at her from time to time and though he often felt her eyes resting on him, she was never the subject of his thoughts and did not for a moment enter into the unbroken reflections aroused by his love for Isabel Bakefield and the dangers which she was incurring.

These dangers he now judged to be less terrible than he had supposed. Since Rolleston's plan consisted in sending Lord Bakefield to a Paris banker to obtain money, it might be assumed that Isabel, held as a hostage, would be treated with a certain consideration, at least until Rolleston, after receiving a ransom, made further demands. But, when this happened, would not he, Simon, be there?

They were now entering a region of a wholly different character, where there was no longer either sand or mud, but a floor of grey rock streaked with thin sheets of hard, sharp-edged stone, which refused to take the imprint of a trail and which even the iron of the horses' shoes failed to mark. Their only chance of information was from the prowlers whom they might encounter.

These were becoming more and more numerous. Two full days had elapsed since the emergence of the new land. It was now the third day; and from all parts, from every point of the sea-side counties or departments, came hastening all who did not fear the risk of the undertaking: vagabonds, tramps, poachers, reckless spirits, daredevils of all kinds. The ruined towns poured forth their contingent of poverty-striken, starving outcasts and escaped prisoners. Armed with rifles and swords, with clubs or scythes, all these brigands wore an air that was both defiant and threatening. They watched one another warily, each of them gauging at a glance his neighbor's strength, ready to spring upon him or ready to act in self-defence.

Simon's questions hardly evoked as much as a grumbling reply:

"A woman tied up? A party? Horses? Not come my way."

And they went on. But, two hours later, Simon was greatly surprised to see the motley dress of three men walking some distance ahead, their shoulders laden with bundles which each of them carried slung on the end of a stick. Weren't those Antonio's Indians?

"Yes," murmured Dolores. "It's Forsetta and the Mazzani brothers." But, when Simon proposed to go after them, "No!" she said, without concealing her repugnance. "They're a bad lot. There's nothing to be gained by joining them."

But he was not listening; and, as soon as they were within hearing, he shouted:

"Is Antonio anywhere about?"

The three men set down their bundles, while Simon and Dolores dismounted and Forsetta, who had a revolver in his hand, thrust it into his pocket. He was a great giant of a fellow.

"Ah, so it's you, Dolores?" he said, after saluting Simon. "Faith, no, Antonio's nowhere hereabouts. We've not seen him."

He smiled with a wry mouth and treacherous eyes.

"That means," retorted Simon, pointing to their burdens, "that you and Mazzani thought it simpler to go hunting in this direction?"

"May be," he said, with a leer.

"But the old professor? Antonio left him in your charge."

"We lost sight of him soon after the *Queen Mary*. He was looking for shells. So Mazzani and I came on."

Simon was losing patience. Dolores interrupted him:

"Forsetta," she said gravely. "Antonio was your chief. We four were fellow-workers; and he asked if you would come with him and me to avenge my uncle's death. You had no right to desert Antonio."

The Indians looked at one another and laughed. It was obvious that notions of right and wrong, promises, obligations, duties of friendship, established rules, decent behavior, all these had suddenly became things which they had ceased to understand. In the stupendous chaos of events, in the heart of this virgin soil, nothing mattered but the satisfaction of the appetites. It was a new situation, which they were unable to analyze, though they hastened to profit by its results without so much as discussing them.

The brothers Mazzani lifted their bundles to their shoulders. Forsetta went up to Dolores and stared at her for a moment without speaking, with eyes that glittered between his half-closed lids. His face betrayed at the same time hesitation and a brutal desire, which he made no attempt to conceal, to seize the girl as his prey.

But he restrained himself and, picking up his bag, moved off with his companions.

Simon had watched the scene in silence. His eyes met Dolores'. She colored slightly and said, in a low voice:

"Forsetta used to know how to keep his distance. . . . The air of the prairie, as you say, has acted on him as it has on the others."

Around them, a bed of dried wrack and other sea-weeds, beneath which the cable disappeared for a length of several miles, formed a series of hills and valleys. Dolores decided that they would halt there and led the horses a little way off, so that they should not disturb Simon's rest.

As it happened, Simon, having lain down on the ground and fallen asleep, was attacked, knocked helpless, gagged and bound before he was able to offer the least resistance to his assailants. These were the three Indians, who had returned at a run.

Forsetta took possession of Simon's pocket-book and watch, tested the firmness of his bonds and then, flat on his stomach, with one of the Mazzanis on either side, crawled under the wrack and seaweed towards the spot where the girl was tending the horses.

Simon repeatedly saw their supple bodies wriggling like reptiles. Dolores, who was busied over the saddle-bags, had her back to them. No feeling of uneasiness warned her of her danger. In vain Simon strove against his bonds and uttered shouts which were stifled by his gag. No power could prevent the Indians from attaining their aim.

The younger Mazzani was the swifter of the two. He suddenly sprung upon Dolores and threw her down, while his brother leapt upon one of the horses and Forsetta, holding another by the bridle, gave his orders in a hoarse tone of triumph:

"Lift her. Take away her rifle. . . . Good! Bring her here. . . . We'll tie her on."

Dolores was placed across the saddle. But, just as Forsetta was uncoiling a rope which he carried round his waist, she raised herself upon the horse's neck, towering over young Mazzani and, raising her arm, struck him full in the chest with her dagger. The Indian fell like a stone against Forsetta; and, when the latter had released himself and made as though to continue the struggle on his own account, Dolores was already before him, threatening him point-blank with her rifle, which she had recovered:

"Clear out," she said. "You too, Mazzani, clear out."

Mazzani obeyed and flew off at a gallop. Forsetta, his features convulsed with rage, withdrew with deliberate steps, leading the second horse. Dolores called to him:

"Leave that horse, Forsetta! This moment . . . or I fire!"

He dropped the bridle and then, twenty paces farther on, suddenly turned his back and fled as fast as he could run.

Simon was impressed not so much by the incident itself—a mere episode in the great tragedy—as by the extraordinary coolness which the girl had displayed. When she came to release him, her hands were cold as ice and her lips quivering:

"He's dead," she faltered. "The young Mazzani is dead. . . ."

"You had to defend yourself," said Simon.

"Yes . . . yes . . . but to take a man's life . . . how horrible! I struck instinctively . . . as though I were acting for the films: you see, we rehearsed this scene a hundred times and more, the four of us, the Mazzanis, Forsetta and I, in the same way, with the words and gestures in the same order. . . . Even to the stab! It was young

Mazzani himself who taught me that; and he often used to say: 'Bravo, Dolores! If ever you play the kidnapping-scene in real life, I'm sorry for your adversary!'"

"Let's hurry," said Simon. "Mazzani may try to avenge his brother's death; and a man like Forsetta doesn't easily give up...."

They continued on their way and once more came upon the cable. Simon went on foot, abreast of Dolores. By turning his head a little, he could see her sad face, with its crown of black hair. She had lost her broad-brimmed hat, as well as her bolero, which was strapped to the saddle of the horse stolen by Mazzani. A silk shirt revealed the modelling of her breasts. Her rifle was slung across her shoulders.

Once more the region of streaked stone extended to the horizon, dotted with wrecks as before and crossed by the wandering shapes of looters. Clouds hung overhead. From time to time there was the humming of an aeroplane.

At noon Simon calculated that they had still twelve or fifteen miles to cover and that therefore they might be able to reach Dieppe before night. Dolores, who had dismounted and, like him, was walking, declared:

"We, yes, we shall get there. But not the horse. He will drop before that."

"No matter!" said Simon. "The great thing is for us to get there."

The rocky ground was now interspersed with tracts of sand where footprints were once more visible; and among other trails were those of two horses coming in their direction along the line of the cable.

"Yet we passed no one on horseback," said Simon. "What do you make of it?"

She did not reply: but a little later, as they reached the top of a slope, she showed him a broad river mingling with the horizon and barring their progress. When they were nearer, they saw that it was flowing from their right to their left; and, when they were nearer still, it reminded them of the stream which they had left that morning. The color, the banks, the windings were the same. Simon, disconcerted, examined the country around to discover something that was different; but the landscape was identical, as a whole and in every detail.

"What does this mean?" muttered Simon. "There must be an inexplicable mirage . . . for, after all, it is impossible to admit that we can have made a mistake."

But proofs of the blunder committed were becoming more numerous. The track of the two horses having led them away from the cable, they went down to the river-bank and there, on a flat space bearing the traces of an encampment, they were compelled to recognize the spot where they had passed the previous night!

Thus, in a disastrous fit of distraction due to the attack by the Indians and the death of the younger Mazzani, both of them, in their excitement, had lost their bearings, and, trusting to the only indication which they had discovered, had gone back to the submarine cable. Then, when they resumed their journey, there had been nothing, no landmark of any kind, to reveal the fact that they were following the cable in the reverse direction, that they were retracing the path already travelled and that they were returning, after an exhausting and fruitless effort, to the spot which they had left some hours ago!

Simon yielded to a momentary fit of despondency. That which was only a vexatious delay assumed in his eyes the importance of an irreparable event. The upheaval of the 4th of June had caused this corner of the world to relapse into absolute barbarism; and to struggle against the obstacles which it presented called for qualities which he did not possess. While the marauders and outcasts felt at home from the beginning in this new state of things, he, Simon Dubosc, was vainly seeking for the solution of the problems propounded by the exceptional circumstances. Where was he to go? What was he to do? Against whom was he to defend himself? How was he to rescue Isabel?

As completely lost in the new land as he would have been in the immensity of the sea, he ascended the course of the river, following, with a distraught gaze, the trace of the two trails marking the sand, which was wet in places. He recognized the prints left by Dolores' sandals.

"It's no use going in that direction," she said. "I explored all the surrounding country this morning."

He went on, however, against the girl's wishes and with no other object than that of acting and moving. And, so doing, in some fifteen minutes' time he came upon a spot where the bank was trampled and muddy, like the banks of a river at a ford.

He stopped suddenly. Horses had passed that way. The mark of their shoes was plainly visible.

"Oh!" he cried, in bewilderment. "Here is Rolleston's trail! . . . This is the distinct pattern of his rubber soles! Can I believe my eyes?"

Almost immediately his quest assumed a more definite form. Fifty yards higher were the traces, still plainly marked, of a camp; and Simon declared:

"Of course! . . . Of course! . . . It was here that they landed last night! Like us, they must have fled before the sudden rise of the water; and like us, they camped on the further side of a hill. Oh," he continued, despairingly, "we were less than a mile from them! We could have surprised them in their sleep! Isn't it frightful to think that nothing told us of it . . . and that such an opportunity. . . ."

He squatted on his heels and, bending over the ground, examined it for some minutes. Then he rose, his eyes met those of Dolores and he said, in a low voice:

"There is one extraordinary thing. . . . How do you explain it?"

The girl's tanned face turned crimson; and he saw that she guessed what he was about to say:

"You came here this morning, Dolores, while I was asleep. Several times your footsteps cover those of our enemies, which proves that you came after they were gone. Why didn't you tell me?"

She was silent, with her eyes still fixed upon Simon's and her grave face animated by an expression of mingled defiance and fear. Suddenly Simon seized her hand:

"But then . . . but then you knew the truth! Ever since this morning, you have known that they went along the river-bank. . . . Look . . . over there . . . you can see their tracks leading eastward. . . . And you never told me! Worse than that. . . . Why, yes . . . it was you who called my attention to the cable. . . . It was you who set me going in a southerly direction . . . towards France. . . . And it is through you that we have lost nearly a whole day!"

Standing close up to her, with his eyes plumbing hers, holding her fingers in his, he resumed:

"Why did you do that? It was an unspeakable piece of treachery.... Tell me, why? You know that I love Miss Bakefield, that she is in the most terrible danger and that to her one day lost may mean dishonor ... and death.... Then why did you do it?"

He said no more. He felt that, in spite of her appearance, which was impassive as usual, the girl was overcome with emotion and that he was dominating her with all the power of his manhood. Dolores' knees were giving way beneath her. There was nothing in her now but submissiveness and gentleness; and, since, in their exceptional position, no reserve could restrain her confession or check her impulsiveness, she whispered:

"Forgive me.... I wasn't thinking ... or rather I thought of no one but you ... you and myself.... Yes, from the first moment of our meeting, the other day, I was swept off my feet by a feeling stronger than anything in this world.... I don't know why.... It was your way of doing things ... your delicacy, when you threw your coat over my shoulders.... I'm not used to being treated like that.... You seemed to me different from the others.... That night, at the Casino, your triumph intoxicated me.... And since then my whole life has been centred on you.... I have never felt like this before.... Men ... men are brutal to me ... violent ... terrible.... They run after me like brutes ... I loathe them.... You ... you ... you're different.... With you I feel a slave.... I want to please you.... Your every movement delights me.... With you I am happier than I've ever been in my life...."

She stood drooping before him, with lowered head. Simon was bewildered at the expression of this spontaneous love, which to him was so completely unforeseen, which was at once so humble and so passionate. It wounded him in his love for Isabel, as though he had committed an offence in listening to the girl's avowal. Yet she spoke so gently; and it was so strange to see this proud and beautiful creature bowing before him with such reverence that he could not but experience a certain emotion.

"I love another woman," he repeated, to set up definitely the obstacle of this love, "and nothing can come between us."

"Yes," she said. "Nevertheless I hoped ... I don't know what.... I had no object in view.... I only wanted us to be alone together, just the two of us, as long as possible. It's over now. I swear it....

We shall find Miss Bakefield. . . . Let me take you to her: I think I shall be better able than you. . . ."

Was she sincere? How could he reconcile this offer of devotion with the passion to which she had confessed?

"What proof have you?" asked Simon.

"What proof of my loyalty? The absolute acknowledgement of the wrong which I have done and which I wish to repair. This morning, when I came here alone, I looked all over the ground to see if there was anything that might give us a clue and I ended by discovering on the edge of this rock a scrap of paper with some writing on it. . . ."

"Have you it?" cried Simon, sharply. "Has she written? Miss Bakefield, I mean?"

"Yes."

"It's for me, of course?" continued Simon, with increasing excitement.

"It's not addressed. But of course it was written for you just as yesterday's message was. Here it is. . . ."

She held out a piece of paper, moist and crumpled, on which he read the following words, hastily scribbled in Isabel's hand:

"No longer making for Dieppe. They have heard a rumor of a fountain of gold . . . a real, gushing spring, it seems. We are going in that direction. No immediate cause for anxiety."

And Dolores added:

"They left before daybreak, going up the river. If this river is really the Somme, we must suppose that they have crossed it somewhere, which will have delayed them. So we shall find them, Simon."

CHAPTER III

SIDE BY SIDE

The jaded horse was incapable of further service. They had to abandon it, after emptying the saddle-bags and removing the rug, which Dolores wrapped about her like a soldier's cloak.

They set out again. Henceforth the girl directed the pursuit. Simon, reassured by Isabel's letter, allowed Dolores to lead the way and twenty times over had occasion to remark her perspicacity and the accuracy of her judgment or intuition.

Then, less anxious, feeling that she understood, he became more talkative and abandoned himself, as on the previous day, to the burst of enthusiasm which the miracle of this new world awakened in him. The still unsettled coast-line, the irresolute river, the changing hues of the water, the ever-varying forms of the heights and valleys, the contours of the landscape, hardly more definite as yet than those of an infant's face: all of this, for an hour or two, was to him a source of wonder and exaltation.

"Look, look!" he cried. "It is as though the landscape were amazed at showing itself in the light of day! Crushed until now beneath the weight of the waters, buried in darkness, it seems embarrassed by the light. Each detail has to learn how to hold itself, to win a place for itself, to adapt itself to new conditions of existence, to obey other laws, to shape itself in accordance with other purposes, in short, to live its life as a thing of earth. It will grow acquainted with the wind, the rain, the frost; with winter and spring; with the sun, the beautiful, glorious sun, which will fertilize it and draw from it all the appearance, color, service, pleasure and beauty which it is capable of yielding. A world is being created before our eyes."

Dolores listened with a charmed expression that spoke of the delight which she felt when Simon spoke for her benefit. And he, all unawares, meanwhile became kindlier and more attentive. The companion with whom chance had associated him was assuming more and more the semblance of a woman. Sometimes he reflected upon the love which she had revealed to him and asked himself whether, in professing her readiness to devote herself, she was not seeking above all to remain by his side and to profit by the circumstances which brought them together. But he was so sure of his own strength and so well protected by Isabel that he took little pains to fathom the secrets of this mysterious soul.

Three times they witnessed murderous conflicts among the swarm of vagabonds who were checked by the barrier of the river. Two men and a woman fell, but Simon made no attempt to defend them or to punish the criminals:

"It is the law of the strongest," he said. "No police! No judges! No executioners! No guillotine! So why trouble ourselves? All social and moral acquisitions, all the subtleties of civilization, all these melt away in a moment. What remains? The primordial instincts, which are to abuse your strength, to take what isn't yours and, in a moment of anger or greed, to kill your fellows. What does it matter? We are back in the troglodyte age! Let each man look to himself!"

The sound of singing reached them from somewhere ahead, as though the river had transmitted its loud echo. They listened: it was a French rustic ditty, sung in a drawling voice to a tuneful air. The sound drew nearer. From the curtain of mist a large open boat came into view, laden with men, women and children, with baskets and articles of furniture, and impelled by the powerful effort of six oars. The men were emigrant sailors, in quest of new shores on which to rebuild their homes.

"France?" cried Simon, when they passed.

"Cayeux-sur-Mer," replied one of the singers.

"Then this river is the Somme?"

"It's the Somme."

"But it's flowing north!"

"Yes, but there's a sharp bend a few miles from here."

"You must have passed a party of men carrying off an old man and a girl bound to two horses."

"Haven't seen anything of that sort," declared the man.

He resumed his singing. Women's voices joined in the chorus; and the boat moved on.

"Rolleston must have branched off towards France," Simon concluded.

"He can't have done that," objected Dolores, "since his present objective is the fountain of gold which some one mentioned to him."

"In that case what has become of them?"

The reply to this question was vouchsafed after an hour's difficult walking over a ground composed of millions upon millions of those broken sea-shells which the patient centuries use in kneading and shaping of the tallest cliffs. It all crackled under their feet and sometimes they sank into it above their ankles. Some tracts, hundreds of yards wide, were covered with a layer of dead fish on which they were compelled to trudge and which formed a mass of decomposing flesh with an intolerable stench to it.

But a slope of hard, firm ground led them to a more rugged promontory overhanging the river. Here a dozen men, grey before their time, clothed in rags and repulsively filthy, with evil faces and brutal gestures, were cutting up the carcass of a horse and grilling the pieces over a scanty fire fed with sodden planks. They seemed to be a gang of tramps who had joined forces for looting on a larger scale. They had a sheep-dog with them. One of them stated that he had that morning seen a party of armed men crossing the Somme, making use of a big wreck which lay stranded in the middle of the river and which they had reached by a frail, hastily-constructed bridge.

"Look," he said, "there she is, at the far end of the cliff. They slid the girl down first and then the old, trussed-up chap."

"But," asked Simon, "the horses didn't get across that way, did they?"

"The horses? They were done for. So they let them go. Two of my mates took three of them and have gone back to France with them. . . . If they get there, it'll be a bit of luck for them. The fourth, he's on the spit: we're going to have our dinner off him. . . . After all, one must eat!"

"And those people, where were they going?" asked Simon.

"Going to pick up gold. They were talking of a fountain flowing with gold pieces . . . real gold coins. We're going too, we are. What we're wanting is arms: arms that are some use."

The tramps had risen to their feet; and, obeying an unconcerted and spontaneous movement, they gathered round Simon and Dolores. The man who had been speaking laid his hand upon Simon's rifle:

"This sort of thing, you know. A gun like that must come in handy just now . . . especially to defend a pocket-book which is probably a fat one. . . . It's true," he added, in a threatening tone, "that my mates and I have got our sticks and knives, for when it comes to talking."

"A revolver's better," said Simon, drawing his from his pocket.

The circle of tramps opened out.

"Stay where you are, will you?" he bade them. "The first of you who moves a step, I shoot him down!"

Walking backwards, while keeping the men covered with his revolver, he drew Dolores to the end of the promontory. The tramps had not budged a foot.

"Come," whispered Simon. "We have nothing to fear from them."

The boat, completely capsized, squat and clumsy as the shell of a tortoise, barred the second half of the river. In foundering she had spilt on the sloping shore a deck cargo of timber, now sodden, but still sound enough to enable Rolleston's gang to build a footbridge twelve yards long across the arm of the river.

Dolores and Simon crossed it briskly. It was easy after that to go along the nearly flat bottom of the keel and to slide down the chain of the anchor. But, just as Dolores reached the ground, a violent concussion shook the chain, of which she had not yet let go, and a shot rang out from the other bank.

"Ah!" she said. "I was lucky: the bullet has struck one of the links."

Simon had faced round. Opposite them, the tramps were venturing on the footbridge one by one.

"But who can have fired?" he demanded. "Those beggars haven't a rifle."

Dolores gave him a sudden push, so that he was protected by the bulk of the wreck:

"Who fired?" she repeated. "Forsetta or Mazzani."

"Have you seen them?"

"Yes, at the back of the promontory. You can understand, a very few words would enable them to make a deal with the tramps and persuade them to attack us."

They both ran round to the other side of the stern. From there they could see the whole of the footbridge and were under cover from the snipers. Simon raised his rifle to his shoulder.

"Fire!" cried Dolores, seeing him hesitate.

The shot rang out. The foremost of the vagabonds fell. He roared with pain, holding his leg. The others hurried back, dragging him with them, and the promontory was cleared of men. But, though the tramps could not risk going on the footbridge, it was no less dangerous for Dolores and Simon to leave the protected area formed by the wreck. Directly they became visible, they were exposed to Forsetta's or Mazzani's fire.

"We must wait till dark," Dolores decided.

For hours, rifle in hand, they watched the promontory, on which a head and shoulders or gesticulating arms appeared at frequent intervals and from which on several occasions also the threat of a levelled rifle forced them to hide themselves. Then, as soon as the darkness was dense enough, they set off again, convinced that Rolleston's trail would continue to ascend the Somme.

They travelled quickly, never doubting that the two Indians and the vagabonds would pursue them. Indeed, they heard their voices across the water and saw fleeting glimmers of light on the same bank as themselves.

"They know," said Dolores, "that Rolleston went in this direction and that we, who are looking for him, are bound to keep to it."

After two hours' progress, during which they groped their way, guided from time to time by the vague shimmering of the river, they reached a sort of isolated chaos into which Simon wearily cast the light of his electric torch. It consisted of enormous blocks of hewn stone, sunk in some lighter, marble, as far as he could see, and partly awash.

"I think we might stop here," said Simon, "at all events till daybreak."

"Yes," Dolores said, "at daybreak you go on again."

He was surprised by this reply:

"But you too, I suppose, Dolores?"

"Of course; but wouldn't it be better for us to separate? Soon Rolleston's trail will leave the river and Forsetta is sure to catch you up, unless I draw him off on another trail."

Simon did not quite understand the girl's plan:

"Then what will you do, Dolores?" he asked.

"I shall go my own way and I shall certainly draw them after me, since it's I they want."

"But in that case you'll fall into the hands of Forsetta and Mazzani, who means to avenge his brother's death. . . ."

"I shall give them the slip."

"And all the brutes swarming in these parts: will you give them the slip too?"

"We're not discussing my affairs, but yours: you have to catch Rolleston. I am hampering your efforts. So let us separate."

"Not at all!" protested Simon. "We have no right to separate; and you may be sure that I shan't leave you."

Dolores' offer aroused Simon's curiosity. What was the girl's motive? Why did she propose to sacrifice herself? In the silence and the darkness, he thought of her for a long while and of their extraordinary adventure. Starting in pursuit of the woman whom he loved, here he was bound by events to another woman, who was herself pursued; and of this other woman, whose safety depended on his and whose fate was closely linked with his own, he knew nothing but the grace of her figure and the beauty of her face. He had saved her life and he scarcely knew her name. He was protecting her and defending her; and her whole soul remained concealed from him.

He felt that she was creeping closer to him. Then he heard these words, which she uttered in a low and hesitating voice:

"It's to save me from Forsetta, isn't it, that you refuse my offer?"

"Of course," he said. "He's terribly dangerous."

She replied, in a still lower voice and in the tone of one making a confession:

"You must not let the threat of a Forsetta influence your conduct. . . . What happens to me is of no great account. . . . Without knowing much about my life, you can imagine the sort of girl I was: a little cigarette-seller hanging about the streets of Mexico; later, a dancer in the saloons at Los Angeles. . . ."

"Hush!" said Simon, placing his hand over her mouth. "There must be no confidences between you and me."

She insisted:

"Still you know that Miss Bakefield is running the same danger as myself. By remaining with me, you sacrifice her."

"Hush!" he repeated, angrily. "I am doing my duty in not leaving you; and Miss Bakefield herself would never forgive me if I did otherwise!"

The girl irritated him. He suspected that she regarded herself as having triumphed over Isabel and that she had been trying to confirm her victory by proving to Simon that he ought to have left her.

"No, no," he said to himself, "it's not for her sake that I'm staying with her. I'm staying because it's my duty. A man does not leave a woman under such conditions. But is she capable of understanding that?"

They had to leave their refuge in the middle of the night, for it was stealthily invaded by the river, and to lie down higher up the beach.

No further incident disturbed their sleep. But in the morning, when the darkness was not yet wholly dispersed, they were awakened by quick, hollow barks. A dog came leaping towards them at such a speed that Simon had no time to do more than pull out his revolver.

"Don't fire!" cried Dolores, knife in hand.

It was too late. The brute turned a somersault, made a few convulsive moments and lay motionless. Dolores stooped over it and said, positively:

"I recognize him, he's the tramps' dog. They are on our track. The dog had run ahead of them."

"But our track's impossible to follow. There's hardly any light."

"Forsetta and Mazzani have their torches, just as you have. Besides, the firing would have told them."

"Then let's be off as quickly as possible," Simon proposed.

"They will catch us up . . . at least, unless you abandon your search of Rolleston."

Simon seized his rifle:

"That's true. So the only thing is to wait for them here and kill them one by one."

"That's so," she said. "Unfortunately. . . ."

"Well?"

"Yesterday, after firing at the tramps, you did not reload your rifle."

"No, but my cartridge-belt is on the sand, at the place where I slept."

"So is mine; and both are covered by the rising water. Therefore there are only the six cartridges of your Browning left."

CHAPTER IV

THE BATTLE

All things considered, their best chance of safety would have been to plunge into the river and escape by the left bank. But this plan, which would have cut them off from Rolleston and which Simon did not wish to adopt except in the last extremity, must have been foreseen by Forsetta, for, as soon as light was clear enough, they saw two tramps going up the Somme on the opposite bank. Under these conditions, how were they to land?

Shortly afterwards, they saw that their retreat was discovered and that the enemy was profiting by their hesitation. On the same bank as themselves, some five hundred yards down-stream, appeared the barrel of a rifle. Up-stream an identical menace confronted them.

"Forsetta and Mazzani," declared Dolores. "We are cut off right and left."

"But there's nobody in front of us."

"Yes, the rest of the tramps."

"I don't see them."

"They are there, believe me, in hiding and well sheltered."

"Let's rush at them and get by!"

"To do that, we should have to cover a bare patch under the cross-fire of Mazzani and Forsetta. They are good shots. They won't miss us."

"Then what?"

"Well, let's defend ourselves here."

It was good advice. The cargo of marble blocks, piled higgledy-piggledy like a child's building-bricks, formed a thorough citadel. Dolores and Simon climbed it and at the top selected a fort, protected on all sides, from which they could see the slightest movements of their enemies.

"They're coming," Dolores declared, after an attentive scrutiny.

The river had deposited along the banks trunks of trees and enormous roots, drifting it was impossible to say whence, which Forsetta and Mazzani were using to cover their approach. Moreover, at each rush forward they protected themselves with broad planks which they carried with them. And Dolores called Simon's attention to the fact that more things were moving across the bare plain; more shields improvised of all sorts of stray materials: coils of rope, broken parts of boats, fragments of pontoons and pieces of boilerplate. All these things were creeping imperceptibly, with the sure, heavy pace of tortoises making for the same goal, along the radius that led to the centre. And the centre was the fortress. The tramps were investing it under the orders of Mazzani and Forsetta. From time to time a limb or a head appeared in sight.

"Ah!" said Simon, in a voice filled with rage. "If only I had a few bullets, wouldn't I stop this inroad of wood-lice!"

Dolores had made a display of the two useless rifles, in the hope that the threatening aspect would intimidate the enemy. But the confidence of the attackers increased with the inactivity of the besieged. It was even possible that the two Indians had scented the ruse, for they scarcely attempted to conceal themselves.

To show his skill, one of them—Forsetta, Dolores declared—shot down a sea-gull skimming along the river. Mazzani accepted the challenge. An aeroplane, humming in their direction and flying lower than most, seemed suddenly to drop from the clouds and silently glided across the river, over the blocks of marble. When it came level, Mazzani threw up his rifle, slowly took aim and fired. The pilot was hit, bore downwards, heeled over on either side alternately, until he seemed about to capsize, and passed on, disappearing in a zig-zag flight like that of a wounded bird.

And suddenly, Simon having shown his head, two bullets fired by the two Indians ricochetted from the nearest stone surface, detaching a few splinters.

"Oh, please don't be so imprudent!" Dolores implored.

A drop of blood trickled down his forehead. She staunched it gently with her handkerchief and murmured:

"You see, Simon, those men will get the better of us. And you still refuse to leave me? You risk your life, though nothing can affect the issue?"

He pushed her away from him:

"My life is not at stake. . . . Nor yours either. . . . This handful of wretches will never get at us."

He was mistaken. Some of the vagabonds were within eighty yards of them. They could hear them talking together; and the men's hard faces, covered with grey stubble, shot up from behind their bucklers like the head of a Jack-in-the-box.

Forsetta was shouting his orders:

"Forward! . . . There's no danger! . . . They've no ammunition! . . . Forward, I tell you! The Frenchman's pockets are stuffed with notes!"

The seven tramps ran forward as one man. Simon levelled his revolver briskly and fired. They stopped. No one was hit. Forsetta was triumphant:

"They're done for! . . . Nothing but short-range Browning bullets! . . . At them!"

He himself, protecting his body with a piece of sheet-iron, ran up at full speed. Mazzani and the tramps formed up in a circle at thirty or forty yards.

"Ready!" bellowed Forsetta. "Out with your knives!"

Dolores remarked to Simon that they must not remain in their observation-post, since most of their enemies would be able to reach the foot of the fortress unseen and slip between the marble blocks. They slid through a gap which formed a chimney from the top to the ground.

"There they are! There they are!" said Dolores. "Fire now! . . . Look, here's a chink!"

Through this chink Simon saw two big ruffians walking ahead of the rest. Two shots rang out. The two big ruffians fell. The party halted for the second time, hesitating what to do.

Dolores and Simon profited by this delay to take refuge at the extreme edge of the river. Three single blocks of marble formed a sort of sentry-box, with an empty space in front of it.

"Charge!" shouted Forsetta, joining the men. "They're trapped! Mazzani and I have got them covered. If the Frenchman stirs, we'll shoot him down!"

THE BATTLE

To meet the charge, Simon and Dolores were obliged to stand up and half-expose themselves. Terrified by the Indian's threat, Dolores threw herself before Simon, making a rampart of her body.

"Halt!" ordered Forsetta, restraining his men's onrush. "And you, Dolores, you leave your Frenchman! Come! He shall have his life if you leave him. He can go: it's you I'm after!"

Simon seized the girl with his left arm and drew her back by main force:

"Not a movement!" he said. "I forbid you to leave me! I'll answer for your safety. As long as I live those brutes shan't get you."

And, with the girl pressed against the hollow of his shoulder, he stretched out his right arm.

"Well done, M. Dubosc!" jeered Forsetta. "Seems that we're sweet on the fair Dolores and that we're sticking to her! Those Frenchmen are all alike! Chivalrous fellows!"

With a wave of the hand he gathered up the tramps for the final attack:

"Now then, mates! One more effort and all the notes are yours! Mazzani and I bag the pretty lady. Is that right, Mazzani?"

All together they came rushing on. All together, at an order from Forsetta, they hurled, like so many projectiles, the pieces of wood and iron with which they had protected themselves. Dolores was not hit, but Simon, struck on the arm, dropped his Browning at the very moment when he had fired at Mazzani and brought him down. One of the tramps leapt upon the pistol, which had rolled away, while Forsetta struggled with Dolores, avoiding the girl's dagger and imprisoning her in his arms.

"Oh, Simon! I'm done for!" she screamed, trying to hang on to him.

But Simon had the five tramps to deal with. Unarmed, with nothing but his hands and feet to fight with, he was shot at three times by the man who had picked up his pistol and was clumsily firing off the last few cartridges. He staggered for a moment under the weight of the other brutes and was thrown to the ground. Two of them seized his legs. Two others tried to strangle him, while the fifth still kept him covered with his empty pistol.

"Simon, save me! . . . Save me!" cried Dolores, whom Forsetta was carrying off, wrapped in a blanket and bound with a rope.

He made a desperate effort, escaping his assailants for a few seconds, and, before they had time to come to close quarters again, acting on a sudden impulse he threw his pocket-book to them, shouting:

"Hands off, you blackguards! Share that between you! Thirty thousand!"

The bundles of notes fell out of the leather wallet and were scattered over the ground. The tramps did not hesitate, but plumped down on their hands and knees, leaving the field to Simon.

Fifty yards away, Forsetta was running along the river, with his prey slung over his shoulder. Farther on, the two tramps posted on the other bank were punting themselves across on a raft which they had found. If Forsetta came up with them, it meant his safety.

"He won't get there," Simon said to himself, measuring the distance with his eye.

With a quick movement, he snatched the knife of one of his aggressors and set off at a run.

Forsetta, who believed him to be still struggling with the vagabonds, did not hurry. He had, so to speak, rolled Dolores round his neck, holding her legs, head and arms in front of him and crushing them to his chest with his rifle and his brawny arms. He shouted to the two men on the raft, to stimulate their ardor:

"Here's the girl! She's my share. . . . You shall have all her jewels!"

The men warned him:

"Look out!"

He turned, saw Simon at twenty paces' distance and tried to throw Dolores to the ground with a heave of the shoulder, like an irksome burden. The girl fell, but she had so contrived matters, under cover of the suffocating blanket, that at the moment of falling she had a good grip on the barrel of the Indian's rifle; and in her fall she dragged him down with her.

The few seconds which Forsetta needed to recover his weapon were his undoing. Simon leapt upon him before he could take aim. He stumbled once more, received a dagger-thrust in the hip and went down on his knees, begging for mercy.

Simon released Dolores' bonds; then, addressing the two tramps who, terror-stricken when on the point of touching ground, were now trying to push off again:

"See to his wound," he ordered. "And there's the other Indian over there: he's probably alive. Look after him too, you shall have your lives."

The tramps were scattering so rapidly in the distance, with Simon's bank-notes, that he gave up all idea of pursuing them.

Thus he remained master of the battle-field. Dead, wounded, or in fight, his adversaries were defeated. The extraordinary adventure was continuing as it were in a savage country and against the most unexpected background.

He was profoundly conscious of the incredible moments through which he was passing, on the bed of the Channel, between France and England, in a region which was truly a land of death, crime, cunning and violence. And he had triumphed!

He could not refrain from smiling and, leaning with both hands on Forsetta's rifle, he said to Dolores:

"The prairie! It's Fenimore Cooper's prairie! The Far West! It's all here: the attack by Sioux, the improvised blockhouse, the abduction, the fight, with the chief of the Pale-Faces coming out victorious! . . ."

She stood facing him, very erect. Her thin silk blouse had been torn in the struggle and hung in strips around her bosom. Simon added, in a tone of less assurance:

"And here's the fair Indian."

Was it emotion, or excessive fatigue after her protracted efforts? Dolores staggered and seemed on the verge of fainting. He supported her, holding her in his arms:

"You're surely not wounded?" he said.

"No. . . . A passing giddiness. . . . I have been badly frightened. . . . And I had no business to be frightened, since you were there and you had promised to save me. Oh, Simon, how grateful I am to you!"

"I have done what any one would have done in my place, Dolores. Don't thank me."

He tried to free himself, but she held him and, after a moment's silence, said:

"She whom the chief calls the fair Indian had a name by which she was known in her own country. Shall I tell you what it was?"

"What was it, Dolores?"

In a low voice, without taking her eyes from his, she replied:

"The Chief's Reward!"

He had felt, in his inner consciousness, that this magnificent creature deserved some such name, that she was truly the prey which men seek to ravish, the captive to be saved at any cost, and that she did indeed offer, with her red lips and her brown shoulders, the most wonderful of rewards.

She had flung her arms about his neck; he was conscious of their caress; and for a moment they stood like that, motionless, uncertain of what was coming. But Isabel's image flashed across his mind and he remembered the oath which she had required of him:

"Not a moment's weakness, Simon. I should never forgive that."

He pulled himself together and said:

"Get some rest, Dolores. We have still a long way to go."

She also recovered herself and went down to the river, where she bathed her face in the cool water. Then, getting to work immediately, she collected all the provisions and ammunition that she could find on the wounded men.

"There!" she said, when everything was ready for their departure. "Mazzani and Forsetta won't die, but we have nothing more to fear from them. We will leave them in the charge of the two tramps. The four of them will be able to defend themselves."

They exchanged no more words. They went up the river for another hour and reached the wide bend of which the people from Cayeux had told them. At the very beginning of this bend, which brought the waters of the Somme direct from France, they picked up Rolleston's trail on a tract of muddy sand. The trail led straight on, leaving the course of the river and running north.

"The fountains of gold lie in this direction evidently," Simon inferred. "Rolleston must be at least a day's journey ahead of us."

"Yes," said Dolores, "but his party is a large one, they have no horses left and their two prisoners are delaying their progress."

They met several wanderers, all of whom had heard the strange rumor which had spread from one end of the prairie to the other and all of whom were hunting for the fountain of gold. No one could give the least information.

But a sort of old crone came hobbling along, leaning on a stick and carrying a carpet-bag with the head of a little dog sticking out of it.

The dog was barking like mad. The old crone was humming a tune, in a faint, high-pitched voice.

Dolores questioned her. She replied, in short, sing-song sentences, which seemed a continuation of her ditty, that she had been walking for three days, never stopping . . . that she had worn out her shoes . . . and that when she was tired . . . she got her dog to carry her:

"Yes, my dog carries me," she repeated. "Don't you, Dick?"

"She's mad," Simon muttered.

The old woman nodded in assent and addressed them in a confidential tone:

"Yes, I'm mad. . . . I used not to be, but it's the gold . . . the rain of gold that has made me mad. . . . It shoots into the air like a fountain . . . and the gold coins and the bright pebbles . . . fall in a shower. . . . So you hold out your hat or your bag and the gold comes pouring into it. . . . My bag is full. . . . Would you like to see?"

She laughed quietly and, beckoning to Simon and Dolores, took her dog by the scruff of the neck, dropped him on the ground and half-opened her bag. Then, again in her sing-song voice:

"You are honest folk, aren't you? . . . I wouldn't show it to any one else. . . . But you won't hurt me."

Dolores and Simon eagerly bent over the bag. With her bony fingers the old woman first lifted a heap of rags kept there for Dick's benefit; she then removed a few shiny red and yellow pebbles. Beneath these lay quite a little hoard of gold coins, of which she seized a generous handful, making them clink in the hollow of her hand. They were old coins of all sizes and bearing all sorts of heads.

Simon exclaimed excitedly:

"She comes from there! . . . She has been there!"

And shaking the mad woman by the shoulders, he asked:

"Where is it? How many hours have you been walking? Have you seen a party of men leading two prisoners, an old man and a girl?"

But the madwoman picked up her dog and closed her bag. She refused to hear. At the most, as she moved away, she said, or rather sang to the air of a ballad which the dog accompanied with his barking:

"Men on horseback.... They were galloping.... It was yesterday.... A girl with fair hair...."

Simon shrugged his shoulders:

"She's wandering. Rolleston has no horses...."

"True," said Dolores, "but, all the same, Miss Bakefield's hair is fair."

They were much astonished, a little way on, to find that Rolleston's trail branched off into another trail which came from France and which had been left by the trampling of many horses—a dozen, Dolores estimated—whose marks were less recent than the bandits' footprints. These were evidently the men on horseback whom the madwoman had seen.

Dolores and Simon had only to follow the beaten track displayed before their eyes on the carpet of moist sand. The region of shells had come to an end. The plain was strewn with great, absolutely round rocks, formed by pebbles agglomerated in marl, huge balls polished by all the submarine currents and deep-sea tides. In the end they were packed so close together that they constituted an insuperable obstacle, which the horsemen and then Rolleston had wheeled round.

When Simon and Dolores had passed it, they came to a wide depression of the ground, the bottom of which was reached by circular terraces. Down here were a few more of the round rocks. Amid these rocks lay a number of corpses. They counted five.

They were the bodies of young men, smartly dressed and wearing boots and spurs. Four had been killed by bullets, the fifth by a stab in the back between the shoulders.

Simon and Dolores looked at each other and then each continued in independent search.

On the sand lay bridles and girth, two nosebags full of oats, half-emptied meat-tins, unrolled blankets and a spirit-stove.

The victims' pockets had been ransacked. Nevertheless, Simon found in a waistcoat a sheet of paper bearing a list of ten names—Paul Cormier, Armand Darnaud, etc.—headed by this note:

"Foret-d'Eu Hunt."

Dolores explored the immediate surroundings. The clues which she thus obtained and the facts discovered by Simon enabled them to reconstruct the tragedy exactly. The horsemen, all members of a Norman hunt, camping on this spot two nights before, had been surprised in the morning by Rolleston's gang and the greater number massacred.

With such men as Rolleston and his followers, the attack had inevitably ended in a thorough loot, but its main object had been the theft of the horses. When these had been taken after a fight, the robbers had made off at a gallop.

"There are only five bodies," said Dolores, "and there are ten names on the list. Where are the other five riders?"

"Scattered," said Simon, "wounded, dying, anything. I daresay we should find them by searching round? But how can we? Have we the right to delay, when the safety of Miss Bakefield and her father is at stake? Think, Dolores: Rolleston has more than thirty hours' start of us and he and his men are mounted on excellent horses, while we. . . . And then where are we to catch them?"

He clenched his fists with rage:

"Oh, if I only knew where this fountain of gold was! How far from it are we? A day's march? Two days'? It's horrible to know nothing, to go forward at random, in this accursed country!"

CHAPTER V

THE CHIEF'S REWARD

During the next two hours they saw, in the distance, three more corpses. Frequent shots were fired, but whence they did not know. Single prowlers were becoming rare; they encountered rather groups consisting of men of all classes and nationalities, who had joined for purposes of defence. But quarrels broke out within these groups, the moment there was the least booty in dispute, or even the faintest hope of booty. No discipline was accepted save that imposed by force.

When one of these wandering bands seemed to be approaching them, Simon carried his rifle ostentatiously as though on the point of taking aim. He entered into conversation only at a distance and with a forbidding and repellent air.

Dolores watched him uneasily, avoiding speech with him. Once she had to tell him that he was taking the wrong direction and to prove his mistake to him. But this involved an explanation to which he listened with impatience and which he cut short by grumbling:

"And then? What does it matter if we keep to the right or to the left? We know nothing. There is nothing to prove that Rolleston has taken Miss Bakefield with him on his expedition. He may have imprisoned her somewhere, until he is free to return for her . . . so that, in following him, I risk the chance of going farther away from her. . . ."

Nevertheless, the need of action drew him on, however uncertain the goal to be achieved. He could never have found heart to apply himself to investigations or to check the impulse which urged him onward.

Dolores marched indefatigably by his side, sometimes even in front. She had taken off her shoes and stockings. He watched her bare feet making their light imprint in the sand. Her hips swayed as she walked, as with American girls. She was all grace, strength and suppleness. Less distracted, paying more attention to external things, she probed the horizon with her keen gaze. It was while doing so that she cried, pointing with outstretched hand:

"Look over there, the aeroplane!"

It was right at the top of a long, long upward slope of the whole plain, at a spot where the mist and the ground were blended till they could not say for certain whether the aeroplane was flying through the mist or running along the soil. It looked like one of those sailing-ships which seem suspended on the confines of the ocean. It was only gradually that the reality became apparent: the machine was motionless, resting on the ground.

"There is no doubt," said Simon, "considering the direction, that this is the aeroplane that crossed the river. Damaged by Mazzani's bullet, it flew as far as this, where it managed to land as best it could."

Now the figure of the pilot could be distinguished; and he too—a strange phenomenon—was motionless, sitting in his place, his head almost invisible behind his rounded shoulders. One of the wheels was half-destroyed. However, the aeroplane did not appear to have suffered very greatly. But what was this man doing, that he never moved?

They shouted. He did not reply, nor did he turn round; and, when they reached him, they saw that his breast was leaning against the steering-wheel, while his arms hung down on either side. Drops of blood were trickling from under the seat.

Simon climbed on board and almost immediately declared:

"He's dead. Mazzani's bullet caught him sideways behind the head. . . . A slight wound, of which he was not conscious for some time, to judge by the quantity of blood which he lost, probably without knowing. . . . Then he succeeded in touching earth. And then . . . then I don't know . . . a more violent hemorrhage, a clot on the brain. . . ."

Dolores joined Simon. Together they lifted the body. No footpads had passed that way, for they found the dead man's papers, watch and pocket-book untouched.

His papers, on examination, were of no special interest. But the route-map fixed to the steering-wheel representing the Channel and the old coast-lines, was marked with a dot in red pencil and the words:

"Rain of gold."

"He was going there too," Simon murmured. "They already know of it in France. And here's the exact place . . . twenty-five miles from where we are . . . between Boulogne and Hastings . . . not far from the Banc de Bassurelle. . . ."

And, quivering with hope, he added:

"If I can get the thing to fly, I'll be there myself in half an hour. . . . And I shall rescue Isabel. . . ."

Simon set to work with a zest which nothing could discourage. The aeroplane's injuries were not serious: a wheel was buckled, the steering-rod bent, the feed-pipe twisted. The sole difficulty arose from the fact that Simon found only inadequate tools in the tool-box and no spare parts whatever. But this did not deter him; he contrived some provisional splices and other repairs, not troubling about their strength provided that the machine could fly for the time required:

"After all," he said to Dolores, who was doing what she could to help him, "after all, it is only a question of forty minutes' flight, no more. If I can manage to take off, I'm sure to hold out. Bless my soul, I've done more difficult things than that!"

His joy once more bubbled over in vivacious talk. He sang, laughed, jeered at Rolleston and pictured the ruffian's face at seeing this implacable archangel descending from the skies. All the same, rapidly though he worked, he realized by six o'clock in the evening that he could scarcely finish before night and that, under these conditions, it would be better to put off the start until next morning. He therefore completed his repairs and carefully tested the machine, while Dolores moved away to prepare their camp. When twilight fell, his task was finished. Happy and smiling, he followed the path on his right which he had seen the girl take.

The plain fell away suddenly beyond the ridge on which the aeroplane had stranded; and a deeper gully, between two sand-hills, led Simon to a lower, basin-shaped plain, in the hollow of which shone a sheet of water so limpid that he could see the bed of black rock at the bottom.

This was the first landscape in which Simon perceived a certain charm, a touch of terrestrial and almost human poetry; and at the far end of the lake there stood the most incredible thing that could be imagined in this region which only a few days earlier had been buried under the sea: a structure which seemed to have been raised by human hands and which was supported by columns apparently covered with fine carving!

Dolores stepped out of it. Tall and shapely, with slow, sedate movements, she walked in to the water, among some stones standing upright in the lake, filled a glass and, bending backwards, drank a few sips. Near by, a trace of steam, rising from a pannikin on a spirit-stove, hovered in the air.

Seeing Simon, she smiled and said:

"Everything's ready. Here's tea, white bread and butter."

"Do you mean it?" he said, laughing. "So there were inhabitants at the bottom of the sea, people who grew wheat?"

"No, but there was some food in that poor airman's box."

"Very well; but this house, this prehistoric palace?"

It was a very primitive palace, a wall of great stones touching one another and surmounted by a great slab like those which top the Druid dolmans. The whole thing was crude and massive, covered with carvings which, when examined closely, were merely thousands of holes bored by molluscs.

"Lithophagic molluscs, Old Sandstone would call them. By Jove, how excited he would be to see these remains of a dwelling which dates thousands and thousands of centuries back and which perhaps has others buried in the sand near it . . . a whole village, I dare say! And isn't this positive proof that this land was inhabited before it was invaded by the sea? Doesn't it upset all our accepted ideas, since it throws back the appearance of men to a period which we are not prepared to admit? Oh, you Old Sandstone, if you were only here! What theories you could evolve!"

Simon evolved no theories. But, though the scientific explanation of the phenomenon meant little to him, how acutely he felt its strangeness and how deeply stirring this moment seemed to him! Before him, before Dolores, rose another age and in circumstances that made them resemble two creatures of that age, the same desolate, barbarous surroundings, the same dangers, the same pitfalls.

And the same peace. From the threshold of their refuge stretched a placid landscape made of sand, mist and water. The faint sound of a little stream that fed the lake barely disturbed the infinite silence.

He looked at his companion. No one could be better adapted to the surrounding scene. She had its primitive charm, its wild, rather savage character and all its mysterious poetry.

The night stretched its veil across the lake and the hills.

"Let us go in," she said, when they had eaten and drunk.

"Let us go in," he said.

She went before, then, turned to give him her hand and led him into the chamber formed by the circle of stone slabs. Simon's lamp was there, hanging from a projection in the wall. The floor was covered with fine sand. Two blankets lay spread.

Simon hesitated. Dolores held him by a firmer pressure of the hand and he remained, despite himself, in a moment of weakness. Besides, she suddenly switched off the lamp and he might have thought himself alone, for he heard nothing more than the infinitely gentle lapping of the lake against the stones upon the beach.

It was then and really not until then that he perceived the snare which events had laid for him by drawing him closer to Dolores during the past three days. He had defended her, as any man would have done, but her beauty had not for a moment affected his decision, or stimulated his courage. Had she been old or ugly, she would have found the same protection at his hands.

At the present moment—he realized it suddenly—he was thinking of Dolores not as a companion of his adventures and his dangers but as the most beautiful and attractive of creatures. He reflected that she, perturbed like himself, was not sleeping either, and that her eyes were seeking him through the darkness. At her slightest movement, the delicate perfume with which she scented her hair, mingled with the warm emanations that floated on the breeze.

She whispered:

"Simon. . . . Simon. . . ."

He did not reply. His heart was oppressed. Several times she repeated his name; then, no doubt believing him asleep, she rose and her naked feet lightly touched the sand. She went out.

What was she going to do? A minute elapsed. There was a sound as of rustling clothes. Then he heard her footsteps on the beach, followed almost immediately by the splash of water and the sound of drops falling in a shower. Dolores was bathing in the darkness.

Simon was next hardly able to detect what was scarcely more perceptible than the swan's gliding over the surface of the pond. The silence and peace of the water remained unbroken. Dolores must have swum towards the centre of the lake. When she returned, he once more heard the pattering of drops and the rustle of clothes while she dressed.

He rose suddenly, with the intention of going out before she entered. But she was quicker than he anticipated and they met on the threshold. He drew back, while she asked him:

"Were you going, Simon?"

"Yes," he said, seeking a pretext. "I am anxious about the aeroplane . . . some thief. . . ."

"Yes . . . yes," she said, hesitatingly. "But I should like first . . . to thank you. . . ."

Their voices betrayed the same embarrassment and the same profound agitation. The darkness hid them from each other's eyes; yet how plainly Simon saw the young woman before him!

"I've behaved as I should to you," he declared.

"Not as other men have done . . . and it is that which touched me. . . . I was struck by it from the beginning. . . ."

Perhaps she felt by intuition that any too submissive words would offend him, for she did not continue her confession. Only, after a moment's pause, she murmured:

"This is our last night alone. . . . Afterwards we shall be parted by the whole of life . . . by everything. . . . Then . . . hold me tight to you for a little . . . for a second. . . ."

Simon did not move. She was asking for a display of affection of which he dreaded the danger all the more because he longed so eagerly to yield to it and because his will was weakening beneath the onslaught of evil thoughts. Why should he resist? What would have been a sin and a crime against love at ordinary times was so no longer at this period of upheaval, when the play of natural forces and of chance gave rise for a time to abnormal conditions of life. To kiss Dolores' lips at such a moment: was it worse than plucking a flower that offers itself to the hand?

They were united by the favoring darkness. They were alone in the world; they were both young; they were free. Dolores' hands were outstretched in despair. Should he not give her his own and obey this delicious dizziness which was overcoming him?

"Simon," she said, in a voice of supplication. "Simon. . . . I ask so little of you! . . . Don't refuse me. . . . It's not possible that you should refuse me, is it? When you risked your life for mine, it was because you had a . . . a feeling . . . a something. . . . I am not mistaken, am I?"

Simon was silent. He would not speak to her of Isabel, would not bring Isabel's name into the duel which they were fighting.

Dolores continued her entreaties:

"Simon, I have never loved any one but you. . . . The others . . . the others don't count. . . . You, the look in your eyes gave me happiness from the first moment. . . . It was like the sun shining into my life. . . . And I should be so happy if there were a . . . a memory between us. You would forget it. . . . It would count for nothing with you. . . . But for me . . . it would mean life changed . . . beautified. . . . I should have the strength to be another woman. . . . Please, please, give me your hand. . . . Take me in your arms. . . ."

Simon did not move. Something more powerful than the impulse of the temptation restrained him: his plighted word to Isabel and his love for her. Isabel's image blended with Dolores's image; and, in his faltering mind, in his darkened conscience, the conflict continued. . . .

Dolores waited. She had fallen to her knees and was whispering indistinct words in a language which he did not understand, words of plaintive passion of whose distress he was fully sensible, and which mounted to his ears like a prayer and an appeal.

In the end she fell weeping at his feet. Then he passed by, without touching her.

The cold night air caressed his features. He walked away at a rapid pace, pronouncing Isabel's name with the fervor of a believer reciting the words of a litany. He turned towards the plateau. When almost there, he lay down against the slope of the hill and, for a long time before falling asleep, he continued to think of Dolores as of some one whose memory was already growing dim. The girl was becoming once more a stranger. He would never know why she had loved him so spontaneously and so ardently; why a nature in which instinct must needs play so imperious a part had found room for such noble feelings, humility and delicacy and devotion.

In the earliest moments of the dawn he gave the aeroplane a final examination. After a few tests which gave him good hopes of success, he went back to the dwelling by the lake. But Dolores was gone. For an hour he searched for her and called to her in vain. She had disappeared without even leaving a footprint in the sand.

On rising above the clouds into the immensity of a clear sky all flooded with sunlight, Simon uttered a cry of joy. The mysterious Dolores meant nothing to him now, no more than all the dangers braved with her or all those which might still lie in wait for him. He had surmounted every obstacle, escaped every snare. He had been victorious in every contest; and perhaps his greatest victory was that of resisting Dolores' enchantment.

It was ended. Isabel had triumphed. Nothing stood between her and him. He held the steering-wheel well under control. The motor was working to perfection. The map and the compass were before his eyes. At the point indicated, at the exact spot, neither too much to the right nor too much to the left, neither overshooting nor falling short of the mark, he would descend within a radius of a hundred yards.

The flight certainly took less than the forty minutes which he had allowed for. In thirty at most he covered the distance, without seeing anything but the moving sea of clouds rolling beneath him in white billows. All he could do now was to fling himself upon it. After stopping his engine, he drew closer and closer, describing great circles. Cries or rather shouts and roars rose from the ground, as though multitudes were gathered together. Then he entered the rolling mist, through which he continued to wheel like a bird of prey.

He never doubted Rolleston's presence, nor the imminence of the fight which would ensue between them, nor its favorable outcome, followed by Isabel's release. But he dreaded the landing, the critical rock on which he might split.

The sight of the ground showing clear of the mist reassured him. A wide and, as it seemed to him, almost flat space lay spread like an arena, in which he saw nothing but four disks of sand which must represent so many mounds and which could be easily avoided. The crowd kept outside this arena, save for a few people who were running in all directions and gesticulating.

At closer quarters, the soil appeared less smooth, consisting of endless sand-colored pebbles, heaped in places to a certain height. He therefore gave all his attention to avoiding collision with these obstacles and succeeded in landing without the slightest shock and in stopping quite quietly.

Groups of people came running about the aeroplane. Simon thought that they wished to help him to alight. His illusion did not last long. A few seconds later, the aeroplane was taken by assault by some twenty men; and Simon felt the barrels of two revolvers pushed against his face and was bound from head to foot, wrapped in a blanket, gagged and deprived of all power of movement, before he could even attempt the least resistance.

"Into the hold, with the rest of them!" commanded a hoarse voice. "And, if he gives trouble, blow out his brains!"

There was no need for this drastic measure. The manner in which Simon was bound reduced him to absolute helplessness. Resigning himself to the inevitable, he counted that the men carrying him took a hundred and thirty steps and that their course brought him nearer to the roaring crowd.

"When you've quite done bawling!" grinned one of the men. "And then make yourselves scarce, see? The machine-gun's getting to work."

They climbed a staircase. Simon was dragged up by the cords that bound him. A violent hand ransacked his pockets and relieved him of his arms and his papers. He felt himself again lifted; and then he dropped into a void.

It was no great fall and was softened by the dense layer of captives already swarming at the bottom of the hold, who began to swear behind their gags.

Using his knees and elbows, Simon made room for himself as best he could on the floor. It must have been about nine o'clock in the morning. From that moment, time no longer counted for him, for he thought of nothing but how to defend the place which he had won against any who might seek to take it from him, whether former occupants or new-comers. Voices muffled by gags uttered furious snarls, or groaned, breathless and exhausted. It was really hell. There were dying men and dead bodies, the death-rattle of

Frenchmen mingling with Englishmen, blood, sticky rags and a loathsome stench of carrion.

During the course of the afternoon, or it might have been in the evening, a tremendous noise broke out, like the sound of a great sheaf of rockets, and forthwith the numberless crowd roared at the top of its voice, with the frenzied fury of an insurgent mob. Then, suddenly, through it all, came orders shouted in a strident voice, more powerful than the tumult. Then a profound silence. And then a crack of sharp, hurried explosions, followed by the frightful rattle of a machine-gun.

This lasted for at least two or three minutes. The uproar had recommenced; and it continued until Simon could no longer hear the fizzing of the fireworks and the din of the shooting. They seemed still to be fighting. They were dispatching the wounded amid curses and shrieks of pain; and a batch of dying men was flung into the hold.

The evening and the night wore through. Simon, who had not touched food since his meal with Dolores beside the lake, was also suffering cruelly from the lack of air, the weight of the dead and the living on his chest, the gag which bruised his jaw and the blanket which wrapped his head like a blind, air-tight hood. Were they going to leave him to die of starvation and asphyxia, in this huddle of sticky, decomposing flesh, above which floated the inarticulate plaint of death?

His bandaged eyes received a feeling as though the day were breaking. His torpid neighbors were swarming like slimy reptiles in a tub. Then, from above, a voice growled:

"No easy job to find him! . . . Queer notions the chief has! As well try and pick a worm out of the mud!"

"Take my boat-hook," said another voice. "You can use it to turn the stiffs over like a scavenger sorting a heap of muck. . . . Lower down than that, old man! Since yesterday morning, the bloke must be at the bottom. . . ."

And the first voice cried:

"That's him! There, look, to the left! That's him! I know my rope around his waist. . . . Patience a moment, while I hook him!"

Simon felt something digging into him that must have been the spike of the boat-hook catching in his bonds. He was hooked, dragged along and hoisted from corpse to corpse to the top of the hold. The men unfastened his legs and told him to stand up:

"Now then, you! Up with you, my hearty!"

His eyes still bandaged, he was seized by the arms and led out of the wreck. They crossed the arena, whose pebbles he felt under foot, and mounted another flight of steps, leading to the deck of another wreck. There the men halted.

From here, when his hood and gag were removed, Simon could see that the arena in which he had landed was surrounded by a wall made of barricades added according to the means at hand: ships' boats, packing-cases and bales, rocks, banks of sand. The hulk of a torpedo-boat was continued by some cast-iron piping. A stack of drain-pipes was followed by a submarine.

All along this enclosure, sentinels armed with rifles mounted guard. Beyond it, kept at a distance of more than a hundred yards by the menace of the rifles and of a machine-gun levelled a little way to the rear, the swarm of marauders was eddying and bawling. Inside, there was an expanse of yellow pebbles, sulphur-colored, like those which the madwoman had carried in her bag. Were the gold coins mixed with those pebbles and had a certain number of resolute, well-armed robbers clubbed together to exploit this precious field? Here and there rose mounds resembling the truncated cones of small extinct volcanoes.

Meantime, Simon's warders made him face about, in order to bind him to the stump of a broken mast, near a group of prisoners whom other warders were holding, like so many animals, by halters and chains.

On this side was the general staff of the gang, sitting for the moment as a court-martial.

In the centre of a circle was a platform of moderate height, edged by ten or a dozen corpses and dying men, some of the latter struggling in hideous convulsions. On the platform a man who was drinking sat or rather sprawled in a great throne-like chair. Near him was a stool with bottles of champagne and a knife dripping with blood. Beside him was a group of men with revolvers in their hands. The man in the chair wore a black uniform relieved with decorations and stuck all over with diamonds and precious stones.

Emerald necklaces hung round his neck. A diadem of gold and gems encircled his forehead.

When he had finished drinking, his face appeared. Simon started. From certain details which recalled the features of his friend Edward Rolleston, he realized that this man was no other than Wilfred Rolleston. Moreover, among the jewels and necklaces, was a miniature set in pearls, the miniature and the pearls of Isabel Bakefield.

CHAPTER VI

HELL ON EARTH

A rascally face was Wilfred Rolleston's, but above all a drunkard's face, in which the noble features of his cousin Edward were debased by the habit of debauch. His eyes, which were small and sunk in their sockets, shone with an extraordinary glitter. A continual grin, which revealed red gums set with enormous, pointed teeth, gave his jaw the look of a gorilla's.

He burst out laughing:

"M. Simon Dubosc? M. Simon Dubosc will pardon me. Before I deal with him, I have a few poor fellows to dispatch to a better world. I shall attend to you in three minutes, M. Simon Dubosc."

And, turning to his henchman:

"First gentleman."

They pushed forward a poor devil quaking with fear.

"How much gold has this one stolen?" he asked.

One of the warders replied:

"Two sovereigns, my lord, fallen outside the barricades."

"Kill him."

A revolver-shot; and the poor wretch fell dead.

Three more executions followed, performed in as summary a fashion; and at each the executioners and their assistants were seized with a fit of hilarity which found expression in cheers and the cutting of many capers.

But when the fourth sufferer's turn came—he had stolen nothing, but was under suspicion of stealing—the executioner's revolver missed fire. Then Rolleston leapt from his throne, uncoiled his great height, towered above his victim's head and buried his knife between his shoulder-blades.

It was a moment of delirious delight. The guard of honor yelped and roared, dancing a frantic jig upon the platform. Rolleston resumed his throne.

After this, an axe cleft the air twice in succession and two heads leapt into the air.

All these monsters gave the impression of the court of some nigger monarch in the heart of Africa. Liberated from all that restrains its impulses and controls its actions, left to itself, with no fear of the police, mankind, represented by this gang of cut-throats, was relapsing into its primitive animal state. Instinct reigned supreme, in all its fierce absurdity. Rolleston, the drink-sodden chieftain of a tribe of savages, was killing for killing's sake, because killing is a pleasure not to be indulged in everyday life and because the sight of blood intoxicated him more effectually than champagne.

"It's the Frenchman's turn"; cried the despot, bursting into laughter. "It's M. Dubosc's turn! And I will deal with him myself!"

He stepped down from his throne again, holding a red knife in his hand, and planted himself before Simon:

"Ah, M. Dubosc," he said, in a husky voice, "you escaped me the first time, in a hotel at Hastings! Yes, it appears I stabbed the wrong man. That was a bit of luck for you! But then, my dear sir, why the deuce, instead of making yourself scarce, do you come running after me . . . and after Miss Bakefield?"

At Isabel's name, he suddenly blazed into fury:

"Miss Bakefield! My *fiancée*! Don't you know that I love her! Miss Bakefield! Why, I've sworn by all the devils in hell that I would bury my knife in the back of my rival, if ever one dared to come forward. And you're the rival, are you, M. Dubosc? But, my poor fool, you shouldn't have let yourself get caught!"

His eyes lit up with a cruel joy. He slowly raised his arm, while gazing into Simon's eyes for the first appearance of mortal anguish. But the moment had not yet come, for he suddenly stayed the movement of his arm and sputtered:

"I have an idea! . . . An idea . . . not half a bad one! . . . No, not half! Look here. . . . M. Dubosc must attend the little ceremony! He will be glad to know that the lot of his dear Isabel is assured. Patience, M. Dubosc!"

He exchanged a few words with his guards, who gave signs of their hearty approval and were at once rewarded with glasses of champagne. Then the preparations began. Three guards marched away, while the other satellites seated the dead bodies in a circle, so as to form a gallery of spectators round a small table which was placed upon the platform.

Simon was one of the gallery. He was again gagged.

All these incidents occurred like the scenes of an incoherent play, stage-managed and performed by madmen. It had no more sense than the fantastic visions of a nightmare; and Simon felt hardly more alarmed at knowing that his life was threatened than he would have felt joy at seeing himself saved. He was living in an unreal world of shifting figures.

The guard of honor fell in and presented arms. Rolleston took off his diadem, as a man might take off his hat in sign of respect, and spread his diamond-studded tunic on the deck, as people might spread flowers beneath the feet of an advancing queen. The three attendants who had been ordered away returned.

Behind them came a woman escorted by two coarse, red-faced viragoes.

Simon shuddered with despair; he had recognized Isabel, but so much changed, so pale! She swayed as she walked, as though her limbs refused to support her and as though her poor distressful eyes could not see plainly. Yet she refused the aid of her companions. A male prisoner followed her, held on a leash like the others. He was an old, white-haired parson.

Rolleston hurried to meet her whom he called his *fiancée*, offering her his hand and leading her to a chair. He resumed his tunic and took his place beside her. The clergyman remained standing behind the table, under the threat of a revolver.

The ceremony, of which the details must have been arranged beforehand, was short. The parson stammered the customary words. Rolleston declared that he took Isabel Bakefield to be his wife. Isabel, when the question was put, bowed her head in assent, Rolleston slipped a wedding-ring upon her finger; then he unfastened from his uniform the miniature set in pearls and pinned it to the girl's bodice:

"My wedding-present, darling," he said, cynically.

And he kissed her hand. She seemed overcome with dizziness and collapsed for a moment, but recovered herself immediately.

"Till this evening, darling," said Rolleston, "when your loving husband will visit you and claim his rights. Till this evening, darling."

He made a sign to the two viragoes to lead their prisoner away.

A few bottles of champagne were opened, the clergyman received a dagger-thrust as his fee and Rolleston, waving his glass and staggering on his legs, shouted:

"Here's the health of my wife! What do you say to that, M. Dubosc? She'll be a lucky girl, eh? To-night makes her King Rolleston's bride! You may die easy, M. Dubosc."

He drew near, knife in hand, when suddenly there broke out, from the arena, a succession of crackling noises, followed by a great uproar. The fireworks were beginning again, as on the night before.

In a moment the scene was changed. Rolleston appeared to sober down at once. Leaning over the side of the wreck, he issued his commands in a voice of thunder:

"To the barricades! Every man to his post! . . . Independent fire! No quarter!"

The deck resounded with the feet of his adherents, who rushed to the ladders. Some, the favored members of the guard of honour, remained with Rolleston. The remaining captives were tied together and more cords were added to the bonds that bound Simon to the foot of the mast.

However, he was able to turn his head and to see the whole extent of the arena. It was empty. But from one of the four craters which rose in the centre a vast sheaf of water, steam, sand and pebbles spurted and fell back upon the ground. In the midst of these pebbles rolled coins of the same color, gold coins.

It was an inconceivable spectacle, reminding Simon of the Iceland geyser. The phenomenon was obviously capable of explanation by perfectly natural causes; but some miraculous chance must have heaped together at the exact spot where this volcanic eruption occurred the treasures of several galleons sunk in times gone by. And these treasures, now dropping like rain on the surface of the earth, must have slipped gradually to the bottom of the huge funnel in which the new forces, concentrated and released by the great upheaval, were boiling over now.

Simon had an impression that the air was growing warmer and that the temperature of this column of water must be fairly high, which fact, even more than fear of the pebbles, explained why no one dared venture into the central zone.

Moreover, Rolleston's troops had taken up their position on the line of the barricades, where the firing had been, furious from the first. The mob of marauders, massed at a hundred yards beyond, had at once given way, though here and there a band of lunatics would break loose from the crowd and rush across the slope. They toppled over, ruthlessly shot down; but others came on, bellowing, maddened by those golden coins which fell like a miraculous rain and some of which rolled to their feet.

These men in their turn spun on their heels and dropped. It was a murderous game, an absolute massacre. The more favored, those who escaped the bullets, were taken prisoners on the line of the barricades and set aside for execution.

And suddenly all grew quiet again. Like a fountain when the water is turned off, the precious sheaf wavered, grew smaller and smaller and disappeared from sight. The troops remaining at the barricades completed the rout of the assailants, while the satellites who made up the guard of honor gathered the gold in rush baskets collected at the fore of the wreck on which Rolleston was performing his antics. The harvest did not take long. The baskets were brought up briskly and the sharing began, a revolting and grotesque spectacle. Eyes burned with greed, hands trembled. The sight, the touch, the sound of the gold drove all these men mad. No famishing beasts of prey, disputing a bleeding quarry, could display greater ferocity and spite. Each man hid his booty in his pockets or in a handkerchief knotted at the corners. Rolleston put his into a canvas bag which he held clasped in his arms:

"Kill the prisoners, the new ones as well as the others!" he shouted, relapsing into drunkenness. "Have them executed! After that, we'll string them all up, so that they can be seen from everywhere and nobody will dare attack us. Kill them comrades! And M. Dubosc to begin with! Who'll attend to M. Dubosc? I haven't the energy myself."

The comrades rushed forward. One of them, more agile than the rest, seized Simon by the throat, jammed his head against the broken mast and, pressing the barrel of his revolver against his temple, fired four times.

"Well done!" cried Rolleston! "Well done!"

"Well done!" cried the others, stamping with rage around the executioner.

The man had covered Simon's head with a strip of cloth already spotted with blood, which he knotted round the mast, so that its ends, brought level with the forehead and turned upwards, looked like a donkey's ear, which provoked an explosion of merriment.

Simon did not feel the least surprise on discovering that he was still alive, that he had not even been wounded by those four shots fired point-blank. This was the way of the incredible nightmare, a succession of illogical acts and disconnected events which he could neither foresee nor understand. In the very article of death, he was saved by circumstances as absurd as those which had led him to death's threshold. An unloaded weapon, an impulse of pity in his executioners: no explanation gave a satisfactory reply.

In any case, he did not make a movement which might attract attention and he remained like a corpse within the bonds which held him fixed in a perpendicular position and behind the veil which hid his face, the face of a living man.

The hideous tribunal resumed its functions and hurried over its verdicts, while washing them down with copious libations. As each victim was condemned, a glass of spirits was served, the tossing off of which was meant to synchronize with a death-struggle. Foul jests, blasphemies, laughter, songs, all mingled in an abominable din which was dominated by Rolleston's piercing voice:

"Now have them hanged. Tell them to string up the corpses! Fire away, comrades! I want to see them dancing at the end of their ropes when I come back from my wife. The queen awaits me! Here's her health, comrades!"

They touched glasses noisily, singing until they had escorted him to the ladder; then they returned and immediately set to work upon the loathsome business which Rolleston had judged necessary to terrorize the distant crowd of marauders. Their jeers and exclamations enabled Simon to follow the sickening incidents of their labors. The dead were hanged, with head or feet downwards alternately, from everything that projected from the ship's deck or its surroundings; and flagstaffs were stuck between their arms, with a blood-soaked rag floating from each.

Simon's turn was approaching. A few dead bodies at most divided him from the executioners, whose hoarse breathing he could hear. This time nothing could save him. Whether he was hanged, or stabbed the moment they saw that he was still alive, the issue was inevitable.

He would have made no attempt to escape, if the thought of Isabel and Rolleston's threats had not exasperated him. He reflected that at that moment Rolleston, the drunkard and maniac, was with the girl who for years had been the object of his desire. What could she do against him? Captive and bound, she was a prey vanquished beforehand.

Simon growled with rage. He contracted his muscles in the impossible hope of bursting his bonds. The period of waiting suddenly became intolerable; and he preferred to draw upon himself the anger of all those brutes and to risk a fight which might at least give him a chance of safety. And would not his safety mean Isabel's release?

Something unexpected, the sensation of a touch that was not brutal but, on the contrary, furtive and cautious, gently persuaded him to silence. A hand behind his back was untying his hands and removing the ropes which held him bound against the mast, while an almost inaudible voice whispered in his ear:

"Not a movement! . . . Not a word! . . ."

The cloth around his head was slowly withdrawn. The voice continued:

"Behave as if you were one of the gang. . . . No one is thinking about you. . . . Do as they do. . . . And, above all, no hesitation!"

Simon obeyed without turning round. Two executioners, not far away, were picking up a corpse. Sustained by the thought that nothing must disgust him if he meant to rescue Isabel, he joined them and helped them to carry their burden and hang it from one of the iron davits.

But the effort exhausted him: he was tortured by hunger and thirst. He turned giddy and was seeking for a support when some one gently seized his arm and drew him toward Rolleston's platform.

It was a sailor, with bare feet and dressed in a blue serge pea-jacket and trousers; he carried a rifle across his back and wore a bandage which hid part of his face.

Simon whispered:

"Antonio!"

"Drink!" said the Indian, taking one of the bottles of champagne; "and look here . . . here's a tin of biscuits. You'll need all your strength. . . ."

After the shocks of the frightful nightmare in which he had been living for thirty-six hours, Simon was hardly capable of surprise. That Antonio should have succeeded in slipping among the gang of criminals accorded, after all, with the logic of events, since the Indian's object was just to be revenged on Rolleston.

"Did you fire at me with a blank cartridge?" asked Simon, "and saved my life?"

"Yes," replied the Indian. "I got here yesterday, when Rolleston was already beginning to drive back the mob of three or four thousand ruffians crowding round the fountains. As he was recruiting all who possessed fire-arms and as I had a rifle, I was enlisted. Since then, I've been prowling right and left, in the trenches which they've dug, in the wrecks, more or less everywhere. I happened to be near his platform when they brought him the papers found on the airman; and I learnt, as he did, that the airman was no other than yourself. Then I watched my opportunity and offered myself as an executioner when it came to a matter of killing you. But I didn't dare warn you in his presence."

"He's with Miss Bakefield, isn't he?" asked Simon anxiously.

"Yes."

"Were you able to communicate with her?"

"No, but I know where she is."

"Let's hurry," said Simon.

Antonio held him back:

"One word. What has become of Dolores?"

He looked Simon straight in the eyes.

"Dolores left me," Simon replied.

"Why?" asked Antonio, in a harsh voice. "Yes, why? A woman alone, in this country: it's certain death! And you deserted her?"

Simon did not lower his eyes. He replied:

"I did my duty by Dolores . . . more than my duty. It was she who left me."

Antonio reflected. Then he said:

"Very good. I understand."

They moved away, unobserved by the rabble of henchmen and executioners. The boat—a Channel packet whose name Simon read on a faded pennant: the *Ville de Dunkerque*; and he remembered that the *Ville de Dunkerque* had been sunk at the beginning of the upheaval—the boat had not suffered much damage and her hull was barely heeling over to starboard. The deck was empty between the funnels and the poop. They were passing the hatch of a companion-way when Antonio said:

"That's Rolleston's lair."

"If so, let's go down," said Simon, who was quivering with impatience.

"Not yet; there are five or six accomplices in the gangway, besides the two women guarding Lord Bakefield and his daughter. Come on."

A little farther, they stopped in front of a large tarpaulin, still soaked with water, which covered one of those frames on which the passengers' bags and trunks are stacked. He lifted the tarpaulin and slipped under it, beckoning to Simon to lie down beside him.

"Look," he said.

The frame contained a skylight protected by stout bars, through which they saw down into the long gangway skirting the cabins immediately below the deck. In this gangway a man was seated with two women beside him. When Simon's eyes had become accustomed to the semidarkness which showed objects somewhat vaguely, he distinguished the man's features and recognized Lord Bakefield, bound to a chair and guarded by the two viragoes whom Rolleston had placed in charge of Isabel. One of these women held in her heavy hand, which pressed on Lord Bakefield's throat, the two ends of a cord passed round his neck. It was clear that a sudden twist of this hand would be enough to strangle the unfortunate nobleman in the space of a few seconds.

CHAPTER VII

THE FIGHT FOR THE GOLD

"Silence!" whispered Antonio, who divined Simon's feeling of revolt.

"Why?" asked Simon. "They can't hear."

"They can. Most of the panes are missing."

Simon continued, in the same low tone:

"But where's Miss Bakefield?"

"This morning I saw her, from here, on that other chair, bound like her father."

"And now?"

"I don't know. But I suppose Rolleston has taken her into his cabin."

"Where's that?"

"He's occupying three or four, those over there."

"Oh," gasped Simon, "it's horrible! And there's no other way out?"

"None."

"Still, we can't. . . ."

"The least sound would be Miss Bakefield's undoing," Antonio declared.

"But why?"

"I am sure of it. . . . All this is thought out. . . . That threat of death to her father; it's blackmail. Besides. . . ."

One of the women moved to a cabin door, listened and returned, sniggering:

"The chit's defending herself. The chief will have to employ strong measures. You're resolved to go through with it, are you?"

"Of course!" said the other, nodding in the direction of her hand. "Twenty quid extra for each of us: it's worth it! On the word of command, pop! And there you are!"

The old man's face remained impassive. His eyes were closed; he appeared to be asleep. Simon was distracted:

"Did you hear? Isabel and Rolleston: she's struggling with him. . . ."

"Miss Bakefield will hold out. The sentence of death has not been issued," said Antonio.

One of the men keeping watch at the entrance to the gangway now came along on his rounds, walking slowly and listening. Antonio recognized him:

"He's one of the original accomplices. Rolleston had all his Hastings stalwarts with him."

The man shook his head:

"Rolleston is wrong. A leader doesn't concern himself like that with trifles."

"He's in love with the girl."

"A funny way of being in love! . . . He has been persecuting her now for four days."

"Why does she refuse him? To begin with she's his wife. She said yes just now."

"She said yes because, ever since this morning, some one has been squeezing dear papa's throat."

"Well, she'll say yes presently so that it shan't be squeezed a little tighter."

The man bent down:

"How's the old chap doing?"

"Impossible to say!" growled the woman, who held the cord. "He told his daughter not to give in, said that he'd rather die. Since then, you'd think he's sleeping. It's two days since he had anything to eat."

"All this sort of thing," retorted the sentry, moving off, "isn't business. Rolleston ought to be on deck. Suppose something happened, suppose we were to be attacked, suppose the enclosure was invaded!"

"In that case, I've got orders to finish the old man off."

"That wouldn't make us come out on top."

A short time elapsed. The two women talked in very low tones. At moments Simon seemed to hear raised voices from the cabin:

THE FIGHT FOR THE GOLD 149

"Listen," he said. "That's Rolleston, isn't it?"

"Yes," said the Indian.

"We must do something, we must do something," said Simon.

The door of the cabin was flung open violently. Rolleston appeared. He shouted angrily to the women:

"Are you ready? Count three minutes. In three minutes strangle him," and, turning round, "You understand, Isabel? Three minutes. Make up your mind, my girl."

He slammed the door behind him.

Quick as thought, Simon had seized Antonio's rifle, but, hampered by the bars, he was unable to take aim before the villain had closed the door.

"You will spoil everything!" said Antonio, crawling from under the tarpaulin and wresting the rifle from him.

Simon, in turn, stood up, with distorted features:

"Three minutes! Oh, poor girl, poor girl!"

Antonio tried to restrain him:

"Let's think of something. There must be a porthole in the cabin."

"Too late. She will have killed herself by then. We must act at once."

He reflected for a moment, then suddenly began to run along the deck and, reaching the hatch of the companion-way, jumped to the bottom. The gangway began with a wider landing where the sentry sat playing cards and drinking.

They rose. One of them commanded:

"Halt! No passage here!"

"All hands on deck! Every man to his post," shouted Simon, repeating Rolleston's words. "At the double! And no quarter! The gold! The rain of gold has started again!"

The men leapt to their feet and made off up the companion. Simon darted down the gangway, ran into one of the two women, whom his shouts had attracted, and flung the same words at her:

"The gold! The rain of gold! Where's the chief?"

"In his cabin," she replied. "Tell him!"

And she made off in her turn.

The other woman, who held the cord, hesitated. Simon felled her with a blow on the point of the chin. Then, without troubling about

Lord Bakefield, he rushed to the cabin. At that moment, Rolleston opened the door, shouting:

"What's up? The gold?"

Simon laid hold of the door to prevent his closing it and saw Isabel, at the back of the cabin, alive.

"Who are you?" asked the villain, uneasily.

"Simon Dubosc."

There was a pause, a respite before the struggle which Simon believed inevitable. But Rolleston fell back, with haggard eyes:

"M. Dubosc? ... M. Dubosc? ... The one who was killed just now?"

"The same," said a voice in the gangway. "And it was I who killed him, I, Antonio, the friend of Badiarinos whom you murdered."

"Ah!" groaned Rolleston, collapsing. "I'm done for!"

He was paralysed by his drunkenness, by his state of stupor and even more obviously by his natural cowardice. Without offering the least resistance, he allowed himself to be knocked down and disarmed by Antonio, while Simon and Isabel rushed into each other's arms.

"My father?" murmured the girl.

"He's alive. Don't be afraid."

Together they went to release him. The old lord was at the end of his forces. It was all that he could do to kiss his daughter and press Simon's hand. Isabel too was on the verge of swooning; shaken with a nervous tremor, she fell into Simon's arms, faltering:

"Oh, Simon, you were just in time. I should have killed myself! ... Oh, what degradation! ... How shall I ever forget?"

Great as was her distress, she had nevertheless the strength to check Antonio's hand when he raised it to stab Rolleston:

"No, please don't. . . . Simon, you agree, don't you. We haven't the right. . . ."

Antonio protested:

"You're wrong, Miss. A monster like that has to be got rid of."

"Please! . . ."

"As you will. But I shall get him again. We have an account to settle, he and I. M. Dubosc, lend me a hand to tie him up!"

The Indian lost no time. Knowing the ruse which Simon had employed to remove the guards, he expected them to return at any moment, no doubt escorted by their comrades. He therefore shoved

Rolleston to the other end of the corridor and bundled him into a dark cupboard.

"Like that," he said, "his accomplices won't find their chief and will look for him outside."

He also bound and locked up the big woman, who was beginning to recover from her torpor. Then, despite the exhausted condition of Lord Bakefield and his daughter, he led them to the companion.

Simon had to carry Isabel. When he reached the deck of the *Ville de Dunkerque*, he was astounded to hear the rattling sounds and to see the great sheaf of pebbles and water spurting towards the sky. By a lucky coincidence, the phenomenon had occurred just as he announced it and caused an excitement by which he had time to profit. Isabel and Lord Bakefield were laid under the tarpaulin, that part of the wreck being deserted. Then Antonio and Simon went to the companion in quest of news. A band of ruffians came pouring down it, shouting:

"The chief! Where's Rolleston?"

Several of them questioned Antonio, who pretended to be equally at a loss:

"Rolleston? I've been hunting for him everywhere. I expect he's at the barricades."

The ruffians streamed back again, scampering up on deck. At the foot of the platform they held a conference, after which some ran towards the enclosing fence, while others, following Rolleston's example, shouted:

"Every man to his post! No quarter! Shoot, can't you, down there?"

"What's happening?" whispered Simon.

"They're wavering," said Antonio, "and giving way. Look beyond the enclosure. The crowd is attacking at several points."

"But they're firing on it."

"Yes, but in disorder, at random. Rolleston's absence is already making itself felt. He was a leader, he was. You should have seen him organize his two or three hundred recruits in a few hours and place each man where he was best suited! He didn't only rule by terror."

The eruption did not last long and Simon had an impression that the rain of gold was less abundant. But it exercised no less attraction upon those whose work it was to collect it and upon others who, no longer encouraged by their leader's voice, were abandoning the barricades.

"Look," said Antonio. "The attacks are becoming fiercer. The enemy feels that the besieged are losing hold."

The slope was invaded from every side; and small bodies of men pushed forward, more numerous and bolder as the firing became less intense. The machine-gun, whether abandoned or destroyed, was no longer in action. The chief's accomplices, who had stood in front of the platform, finding themselves unable to enforce their authority and restore discipline, leapt into the arena and ran to the trenches. They were the most resolute of the defenders. The assailants hesitated.

So, for two hours, fortunes of the fight swayed to and fro. When night fell, the battle was still undecided.

Simon and Antonio, seeing the wreck deserted, collected the necessary arms and provisions. They intended to prepare for flight at midnight, if circumstances permitted. Antonio went off to reconnoitre, while Simon watched over the repose of his two patients.

Lord Bakefield, although fit to travel, was still badly pulled down and slept, though his sleep was disturbed by nightmares. But Simon's presence restored to Isabel all her energy, all her vitality. Sitting side by side, holding each other's hands, they told the story of those tragic days; and Isabel spoke of all that she had suffered, of Rolleston's cruelty, of his coarse attentions to her, of the constant threat of death which he held over Lord Bakefield if she refused to yield, of the nightly orgies in camp, the bloodshed, the tortures, the cries of the dying and the laughter of Rolleston's companions. . . .

She shuddered at certain recollections, nestling against Simon as though she feared to find herself once more alone. All around them was the flash of fire-arms and the rattle of shots which seemed to be coming nearer. A din at once confused and terrific, made up of a hundred separate combats, death-struggles and victories, hovered above the dark plain, over which, however, a pale light appeared to be spreading.

Antonio returned in an hour's time and declared that flight was impossible:

"Half the trenches," he said, "are in the hands of the assailants, who have even penetrated into the enclosure. And they won't let any one pass, any more than the besieged will."

"Why?"

"They're afraid of gold being taken away. It seems that there's a sort of discipline among them and that they're obeying leaders whose object is to capture from the besieged the enormous booty which they have accumulated. And, as the assailants are ten or even twenty to one, we must expect a wholesale massacre!"

The night was full of tumult. Simon observed that the dense layer of clouds was breaking up in places and that gleams of light were falling from the starry sky. They could see figures darting across the arena. Two men first, then a number of others boarded the *Ville de Dunkerque* and went down the nearest companion way.

"Rolleston's accomplices returning," murmured Antonio.

"What for? Are they looking for Rolleston?"

"No, they think he's dead. But there are the bags, the bags filled with coin, and they are all going to fill their pockets."

"The gold is there, then?"

"In the cabins. Rolleston's share on one side; his accomplices on the other."

Below deck quarrels were beginning, followed almost immediately by a general affray, which was punctuated by yells and moans. One by one the victors emerged from the companion way. But shadows crept down it all night long; and the newcomers were heard searching and destroying.

"They'll find Rolleston in the end," said Simon.

"I don't care if they do," said Antonio, with a grin which Simon was to remember thereafter.

The Indian was getting together their arms and ammunition. A little before daybreak, he awoke Lord Bakefield and his daughter and gave them rifles and revolvers. The final assault would not be long delayed; and he calculated that the *Ville de Dunkerque* would be the immediate objective of the assailants and that it would be better not to linger there.

The little party therefore set out when the first pale gleams of dawn showed in the sky. They had not set foot on the sand of the arena before the signal for the attack was given by a powerful voice which sounded from the bulk of the submarine; and it so happened that, at the very moment when the final offensive was launched, when the besieged, better armed than the attackers, were taking measures of defense which were also better organized, the roar of the eruption rent the air with its thousand explosions.

Then and there, the enemy's onslaught became more furious, and the besieged began to retreat, as Simon and Antonio perceived from the disorderly rush of men falling back like trapped animals, seeking cover behind which to defend themselves or hide.

In the middle of the arena, the scorching rain and the showers of falling pebbles created a circular empty space; nevertheless, some of the more desperate assailants were bold enough to venture into it and Simon had a fleeting vision in which he seemed to see—but was it possible?—Old Sandstone running this way and that under a strange umbrella made of a round sheet of metal with the edge turned down.

The mob of invaders was growing denser. They collided with groups of men and women, brandishing sticks, old swords, scythes, hill-hooks and axes, who fell upon the fugitives. Simon and Antonio were twice obliged to take part in the fighting.

"The position is serious," said Simon, taking Isabel aside. "We must risk all for all and try to find a way through. Kiss me, Isabel, as you did on the day of the shipwreck."

She gave him her lips, saying:

"I have absolute faith in you, Simon."

After many efforts and two brushes with some ruffians who tried to stop them, they reached the line of the barricades and crossed it without hindrance. But in the open space outside they met fresh waves of marauders breaking furiously against the defences, including parties of men who seemed to be running away, rather than pursuing a quarry. It was as though they themselves were threatened by some great danger. Fierce and murderous for all that, they plundered the dead and wildly attacked the living.

"Look out!" cried Simon.

It was a band of thirty or forty street-boys and hooligans, among whom he recognized two of the tramps who had pursued him. At sight of Simon, they egged on the gang under their command.

By some ill chance Antonio slipped and fell. Lord Bakefield was knocked down. Simon and Isabel, caught in an eddy, felt that they were being stifled by a mass of bodies whirling about them. Simon, however, succeeded in seizing hold of her and levelling his revolver. He fired three times in succession. Isabel did likewise. Two men dropped. There was a moment's hesitation; then a new onslaught separated the lovers.

"Simon, Simon!" cried the terrified girl.

One of the tramps roared:

"The girl! Carry her off! She'll fetch her weight in gold!"

Simon tried to reach her. Twenty hands opposed his desperate efforts; and, while defending himself, he saw Isabel pushed towards the barricades by the two tramps. She stumbled and fell. They were trying to raise her when suddenly two shots rang out and both fell headlong.

"Simon! Antonio!" cried a voice.

Through the fray Simon saw Dolores, sitting erect on a horse all covered with foam. Her rifle was levelled and she was firing. Three of the nearest aggressors were struck. Simon contrived to break away, run to Isabel and join Dolores, to whom Antonio at the same time was bringing Lord Bakefield.

Thus the four were together again, but each was followed by the rabble of persistent marauders, and these were reinforced by dozens of others, who loomed out of the fog and doubtless imagined that the stake in such a battle, in which the number of their opponents was so small, must be the capture of some treasure.

"There are more than a hundred of them," said Antonio. "We are done for."

"Saved!" cried Dolores, who now ceased firing.

"Why?"

"Yes, we must hold out . . . one minute. . . ."

Dolores' reply was drowned in the uproar. Their assailants came along with a rush. With their backs against the horse, the little party faced in all directions, firing, wounding, killing. With his left hand Simon discharged his revolver, while with his right hand, which gripped his rifle by the barrel, whirling it to terrible effect, he held the enemy at a distance.

But how could they resist the torrent, continually renewed, that rushed upon them. They were submerged. Old Lord Bakefield was struck senseless with a stick; and one of Antonio's arms was paralysed by a blow from a stone. Any further resistance was out of the question. The hideous moment had come when people fall, when their flesh is trampled underfoot and torn asunder by the enemy's claws.

"Isabel!" murmured Simon, crushing her passionately in his arms.

They dropped to their knees together. The beasts of prey fell upon them, covering them with darkness.

A bugle sounded some distance away, scattering its lively notes upon the air. Another call rang out in reply. It was a French bugle sounding the charge.

A great silence, heavy with fear, petrified the hoardes of pillagers. Simon, who was losing consciousness, felt that the weight above him was lightened. Some of the beasts of prey were taking flight.

He half-raised himself, while supporting Isabel, and the first thing that struck him was Antonio's attitude. The Indian, with drawn face, was gazing at Dolores. Slowly and steadily he took a few steps towards her, like a cat creeping up to its prey, and suddenly, before Simon could intervene, he leapt on the crupper behind her, passed his arms under hers and dug his heels into the horse, which broke into a gallop along the barricades, towards the north.

From the opposite direction, through the mist, appeared the sky-blue uniforms of France.

CHAPTER VIII

THE HIGH COMMISSIONER FOR THE NEW TERRITORIES

"My fault! . . . Now aren't you convinced, as I am, that this is a ramification of my fault, ending in a *cul-de-sac*? So that all the eruptive forces immobilized in the direction of this blind alley have found a favorable position . . . so that all these forces . . . you grasp the idea, don't you?"

Simon grasped it all the less inasmuch as Old Sandstone was becoming more and more entangled in his theory, while he, Simon, was wholly absorbed in Isabel and had ears for hardly anything but what she was telling him.

They were all three a little way outside the barricades, among the groups of tents around which the soldiers, in overalls, and fatigue-caps, were moving to and fro and preparing their meals. Isabel's face was already more peaceful and her eyes less uneasy. Simon gazed at her with infinite tenderness. In the course of the morning the fog had at last dispersed. For the first time since the day when they had travelled together on the deck of the *Queen Mary*, the sun shone in a cloudless sky; and one might almost have thought that nothing had occurred between that day and this to divide them. All evil memories faded away. Isabel's torn dress, her pallor and her bruised wrists were the reminder merely of an adventure already remote, since the glorious future was opening out before them.

Inside the barricades, a few soldiers scurried round the arena, stacking the dead bodies, while others, farther back, stationed on the wreck of the *Ville de Dunkerque*, removed the sinister shapes hanging from their gibbets. Near the submarine, in an enclosed space guarded by many sentries, some dozens of prisoners were herded and were joined at every moment by fresh batches of captives.

"Of course," resumed Old Sandstone, "there are many other obscure points; but I shall not leave this until I have studied all the causes of the phenomenon."

"And I," said Simon, laughing, "should very much like to know how you managed to get here."

This was a question which possessed little interest for Old Sandstone, who replied, vaguely:

"How do I know! I followed a crowd of good people. . . ."

"Good looters and murderers!"

"Oh, do you think so? Yes, it may be . . . it seemed to me, sometimes. . . . But I was so absorbed! So many observations to make! Besides, I was not alone . . . at least, on the last day."

"Really? Who was with you?"

"Dolores. We made the whole of the last stage together; and it was she who brought me here. She left me when we came in sight of the barricades. For that matter, it was impossible to enter this enclosure and examine the phenomena more closely. Directly I went forward, pom-pom went the machine-gun! At last, suddenly, the crowd burst the dike. But what puzzles me now is that these eruptions seem already to be decreasing in violence, so that we can foresee the end of them very shortly. True, on the other hand. . . ."

But Simon was not listening. He had caught sight, in the arena, of the captain commanding the detachment, with whom he had not been able to exchange more than a few words that morning, as the officer had at once gone in pursuit of the fugitives. Simon led Isabel to the tent, set aside for her, in which Lord Bakefield was resting, and joined the captain, who cried:

"We are straightening things out, M. Dubosc. I've sent a few squads north; and all these bands of cut-throats will fall into my hands or into those of the English troops, who, I'm told, have arrived. But what savages! And how glad I am that I came in time!"

Simon thanked him in the name of Lord Bakefield and his daughter.

"It's not I whom you should thank," he replied, "but that strange woman, whom I know only by the name of Dolores, and who brought me here."

The captain related how he had been operating since three o'clock in the out-posts of Boulogne, where he was garrisoned, when he received from the newly-appointed military governor an order instructing him to move towards Hastings, to take possession of the country as far as mid-way between the two coasts and to put down all excesses ruthlessly.

"Well, this morning," he said, "when we were patrolling two or three miles from there, I saw the woman ride up at a gallop. She told me in a few words what was happening inside these barricades, which she had not been able to pass, but behind which Simon Dubosc was in danger. Having succeeded in catching a horse, she had come to beg me to go to your assistance. You can imagine how quickly I marched in the direction she gave me, as soon as I heard the name of Simon Dubosc. And you will understand also why, when I saw that she in her turn was in danger, I rushed in pursuit of the man who was carrying her off."

"What then, captain?"

"Well, she returned, quite quietly, all alone on her horse. She had thrown the Indian, whom my men picked up in the neighborhood, rather the worse for his fall. He says he knows you."

Simon briefly related the part which Antonio had played in the tragedy.

"Good!" cried the officer. "The mystery is clearing up!"

"What mystery, captain?"

"Oh, something quite in keeping with all the horrors that have been committed!"

He drew Simon to the wreck and down, the companion-ladder.

The wide gangway was littered with empty bags and baskets. All the gold had disappeared. The doors of the cabins occupied by Rolleston had been demolished. But, outside the last of these cabins and a little before the cupboard into which Antonio had locked Rolleston on the previous evening, Simon, by the light of an electric torch switched on by the officer, saw a man's body hanging from the ceiling. The knees had been bent back and fastened to keep the feet from touching the floor.

"There's the wretched Rolleston," said the captain. "Obviously he has got no more than his deserts. But, all the same. . . . Look closely. . . ."

He threw the rays of the lamp over the upper part of the victim's body. The face, covered with black clotted blood, was unrecognizable. The drooping head displayed the most hideous wound: the skull was stripped of its skin and hair.

"It was Antonio who did that," said Simon, remembering the Indian's smile when he, Simon, had expressed the fear that the ruffians might succeed in finding and releasing their chief. "After the fashion of his ancestors, he has scalped the man whom he wished to punish. I tell you, we're living in the midst of savagery."

A few minutes later, on leaving the wreck, they saw Antonio who was talking to Dolores near the spot where the submarine strengthened the former line of defence. Dolores was holding her horse by the bridle. The Indian was making gestures and seemed to be greatly excited.

"She's going away," said the officer. "I've signed a safe-conduct for her."

Simon crossed the arena and went up to her:

"You're going, Dolores?"

"Yes."

"Where?"

"Where my horse chooses to take me . . . and as far as he can carry me."

"Won't you wait a few minutes?"

"No."

"I should have liked to thank you. . . . So would Miss Bakefield. . . ."

"Miss Bakefield has my best wishes!"

She mounted. Antonio snatched at the bridle, as though determined to detain her, and began to speak to her in a choking voice and in a language which Simon did not understand.

She did not move. Her beautiful, austere face did not change. She waited, with her eyes on the horizon, until the Indian, discouraged, released the bridle. Then she rode away. Not once had her eyes met Simon's.

She rode away, mysterious and secretive to the last. Simon's refusal, his conduct during the night which they had passed in the prehistoric dwelling must have humiliated her profoundly; and the best proof was this departure without farewell. But, on the other hand, what miracles of dogged heroism she must have wrought to cross this sinister region by herself and to save not only the man who had spurned her but the woman whom that man loved above all things in this world!

A hand rested on Simon's shoulder:

"You, Isabel!" he said.

"Yes. . . . I was over there, a little farther on. . . . I saw Dolores go."

The girl seemed to hesitate. At length, she murmured, watching him attentively:

"You didn't tell me she was so strikingly beautiful, Simon."

He felt slightly embarrassed. Looking her straight in the eyes, he replied:

"I had no occasion to tell you, Isabel."

At five o'clock that afternoon, the French and British troops being now in touch, it was decided that Lord Bakefield and his daughter should make part of an English convoy which was returning to Hastings and which had a motor-ambulance at its disposal. Simon took leave of them, after asking Lord Bakefield's permission to call on him at an early date.

Simon considered that his mission was not yet completed in these days of confusion. Indeed, before the afternoon was over, an aeroplane alighted in sight of the camp and the captain was asked to send immediately reinforcements, as a conflict appeared inevitable between the French and a British detachment, both of which had planted their colors on a ridge overlooking the whole country. Simon did not hesitate for a moment. He took his place between the two airmen.

It is needless to describe in all its details the part which he played in this incident, which might have had deplorable results: the way in which he threw himself between the adversaries, his entreaties, his threats and, at last, the order to withdraw which he gave to the French with such authority and such persuasive force. All this is history; and it is enough to recall the words uttered two days later by the British prime minister in the House of Commons:

"I have to thank M. Simon Dubosc. But for him, there would have been a stain upon our country's honor; French blood would have been shed by English hands. M. Simon Dubosc, the wonderful man who crossed what was once the Channel at one stride, understood that it would be necessary, at least for a few hours, to exercise a little patience towards a great nation which for so many centuries has been accustomed to feel that it was protected by the seas and which suddenly found itself disarmed, defenceless, deprived of its natural ramparts. Let us not forget that Germany, that very morning, with her customary effrontery, offered France an alliance and proposed the immediate invasion of Great Britain by the whole of the united forces of the two countries. *Britannia delenda est!* Mr. Speaker, it was Simon Dubosc who gave the reply, by achieving the miracle of a French retreat! All honor to Simon Dubosc!"

France at once recognized Simon's action by appointing the young man high commissioner for the new French territories. For four days longer he was ubiquitous, flying over the province which he had conquered, restoring order, enforcing harmony, discipline and security. Pursued and captured, all the bands of pillagers and spoilers were duly brought to trial. Aeroplanes sailed the heavens. Provision-lorries ran in all directions, assuring travellers the means of transport. Chaos was becoming organized.

At last one day, Simon called at Lord Bakefield's country-house near Battle. Here too tranquillity had returned. The servants had resumed their duties. Only a few cracks in the walls, a few gaps in the lawns reminded them of the hours of terror.

Lord Bakefield, who appeared to be in excellent health, received Simon in the library and gave him the same cordial welcome as on the Brighton golf-links:

"Well, young man, where do we stand now?"

"On the twentieth day after my request for your daughter's hand," said Simon, smiling, "and as you gave me twenty days in which to perform a certain number of exploits, I come to ask you, on the appointed date, whether I have, in your opinion, fulfilled the conditions settled between us."

Lord Bakefield offered him a cigar and handed him a light.

He made no further reply. Simon's exploits and his rescue of Lord Bakefield when at the point of death, these obviously were interesting things, deserving the reward of a good cigar, with Isabel's hand perhaps thrown into the bargain. But it was asking too much to expect thanks as well and praise and endless effusions. Lord Bakefield remained Lord Bakefield and Simon Dubosc a nobody.

"Well, see you later, young man . . . Oh, by the way! I have had the marriage annulled which that reptile Rolleston forced upon Isabel. . . . The marriage wasn't valid of course; but I've done what was necessary just as though it had been. Isabel will tell you all about it. You'll find her in the park."

She was not in the park. She had heard that Simon had called and was waiting for him on the terrace.

He told her of his interview with Lord Bakefield.

"Yes," she said, "my father accepts the position. He considers that you have satisfied the ordeal."

"And you, Isabel?"

She smiled:

"I have no right to be more difficult than my father. But remember that there were not only his conditions: there was one added by myself."

"Which condition was that, Isabel?"

"Have you forgotten? . . . On the deck of the *Queen Mary*?"

"Then, Isabel, you doubt me?"

She took both his hands and said:

"Simon, it sometimes makes me rather sad to think that in this great adventure it was not I but another who was your companion in danger, the one whom you defended and who protected you."

He shook his head:

"No, Isabel, I never had but one companion, you, Isabel, and you alone. You were my only aim and my only thought, my one hope and my one desire."

After a moment's reflection, she said:

"I talked of her a good deal with Antonio, on the way home. Do you know, Simon, that girl is not only very beautiful, but capable of the noblest, loftiest feelings? I know nothing of her past; according to Antonio, it had its unsettled moments. But since then . . . since then . . . in spite of her present mode of life, in spite of all the admiration which she attracts, she leads an existence apart. You alone have really stirred her feelings. For you, from what I can see for myself and from what Antonio told me—and he, after all, is only a rejected and embittered lover—for you Dolores would have laid down her life and that from the first day. Did you know that, Simon?"

He was silent.

"You are right," she said. "You can't answer. However, there is one point, Simon, on which I ask you to tell me the absolute truth.

I can look you straight in the face, can I not? There is not in the depths of your being a single memory that comes between us? . . . Not a weakness? . . . Not a disloyal thought?"

He pressed her to him and, with his lips on hers, said:

"There's you, Isabel, and you alone; you in the past and you in the future."

"I believe you, Simon," she declared.

The wedding took place a month later; and they went to live in the wreck of the *Ville de Dunkerque*, the official residence of the French high commissioner of the new territories.

It was here that the draft agreement was signed, in accordance with Simon Dubose's proposal and his preliminary investigations, for the great canal which was to bisect the Isthmus of Normandy, allotting to each country, right and left, an almost equal portion of land.

Here too was signed the solemn covenant by which Great Britain and France declared eternal friendship and laid the foundations of the United States of Europe.

And it was here that four children were born to Isabel and Simon.

In after years, Simon often went on horseback or by aeroplane, accompanied by his wife, to visit his friend Edward Rolleston. When he had recovered from his wounds, Rolleston set to work and became the manager of a large fishing-industry on the new English coast, in which he employed Antonio. Rolleston married. The Indian lived alone for a long time, waiting for her who never came and of whom no one ever spoke. But one day he received a letter and went away. Some months later, he wrote from Mexico announcing his marriage to Dolores.

But Isabel and Simon's favorite walk led them to Old Sandstone's house. He lived in a little bungalow, close to the prehistoric dwelling by the lake, where he pursued his researches into the new land. The showers of gold, now exhausted, no longer interested him; moreover, the problem had been solved. But what an indecipherable riddle was this building, standing on a site of the Eocene period!

"There were apes in those days," Old Sandstone declared. "There's no doubt of that. But men! And men capable of building, of ornamenting their dwellings of carving stone! No, I confess this is a phenomenon which unsettles all one's ideas. What do you make of it, Simon?"

Simon made no reply. A boat was rocking on the lake. He took his place in it with Isabel and rowed with a care-free mind; nor did Dolores' image ever rise from this limpid water, in which she had bathed on a certain voluptuous evening. Simon was the husband of one alone and this was the woman whom he had won.

THE END

SEAWOLF PRESS

Detective Books From SeaWolf Press

Arsène Lupin 100ᵗʰ Anniversary Collection

- Arsène Lupin, Gentleman-Burglar
- Arsène Lupin versus Herlock Sholmes
- The Hollow Needle
- 813
- The Crystal Stopper
- Confessions of Arsène Lupin
- The Teeth of the Tiger
- The Woman of Mystery
- The Golden Triangle
- The Secret of Sarek
- The Eight Strokes of the Clock
- The Secret Tomb

Agatha Christie 100ᵗʰ Anniversary Collection

- The Mysterious Affair at Styles
- The Secret Adversary
- The Murder on the Links
- The Man in the Brown Suit
- The Secret of the Chimneys

See our complete catalog at www.SeaWolfPress.com

Made in the USA
Las Vegas, NV
23 September 2023